BALANCE PETER GIGLIO

PETER GIGLIO BALANCE

Evil Jester Press

NEW YORK

PETER GIGLIO

<u>Novels</u>

Anon
The Dark (With Scott Bradley)

<u>Novellas</u>

A Spark in the Darkness
Balance

<u>Edited by</u>

Help! *Wanted: Tales of On-the-Job Terror*
Evil Jester Digest: Volume One

ABOUT THE AUTHOR

Peter Giglio is a Pushcart Prize nominated novelist, screenwriter, and anthologist. He is the author of two published novels—*Anon* and *The Dark* (with Scott Bradley)—and two published novellas—*A Spark in the Darkness* and *Balance*. His short stories can be found in several anthologies, including *Werewolves and Shapeshifters: Encounters with the Beast Within*, edited by John Skipp, and *Live and Let Undead*, edited by Hollie Snider. He is also the editor of the anthology Help! *Wanted: Tales of On-the-Job Terror*, featuring Stephen Volk, Joe McKinney, Jeff Strand, Gary Brandner, Amy Wallace, Lisa Morton, among others. Peter is currently shopping—with co-writer Scott Bradley—a feature-length, screen adaptation of Joe R. Lansdale's "The Night They Missed the Horror Show."

Peter Giglio, Balance, & Native Grace
—An Introduction by Eric Shapiro—

Introductions are long blurbs, essentially.

The introducer exists to praise the introduced. The ritual, in its purest form, is a type of celebration; one artist publicly high-fiving another. Cronyism is on display, as well. The introducer says, loud and clear, "I stand with this guy. And you should, too!"

The introducer doesn't even have to be known. His or her mere function elevates both introducer and introduced alike. As with a blurb, everybody wins.

But where does the reader fit in? Personally, when I'm reading introductions, I like to fantasize that I'm the one being introduced. Same with blurbs. I read that stuff and whisper to myself, "Why, yes. This could be *me* they're talking about..."

Is this what everybody does? I hope so! Otherwise, color me embarrassed.

Sometimes, though, all of the above becomes background. Sometimes, when one author introduces another, the elements of praise, high-fiving, cronyism, and reader fantasy take a backseat to two compelling factors: (1) The book actually being excellent, and (2) (accordingly) the introduction actually making way for something special.

As it happens, these compelling factors exist here today. And there's not just "something" special on hand; there are two special things. One is *Balance*; the other is its author, Peter Giglio (more of a person than a thing, I should make clear).

Since we're all now involved in an introduction, the natural topic is one of Quality. Which begs the question: What Is Quality? What makes something good?

Relax, I won't even attempt an explanation. That shit could go on forever...

What I will say is that Peter Giglio knows. He knows what's good. He feels it in his solar plexus. And can we all just pause for a moment and meditate upon how rare that is?

Authors are an amusing breed. You've got your snobs and your cynics and your basic egomaniacs. You've got your left-brainers, your right-brainers, and your empty-headed hacks. All of them have a certain attitude; be generic and call it The Author's Attitude. It's a look in the eye. It says to you, "I Know What I'm Talking About."

But fuck all that. Most of them don't know. Most of their work is second-rate at best. Most of it, I don't even care to keep on reading after paragraph one.

Giglio's rare; he knows what he's talking about. He knows how to get you fused to the page. He knows how to massage, finesse, and dance with every sentence 'til it's capable of tangling itself around you like a snake, then either kissing or biting you (his choice) by the time it punctuates. He's got what Orwell called "native grace"—which is an elegant way of saying that he's talented.

I was born in 1978. Since then, the meaning of talent has changed. Sure, we've got our pop idol TV contests, and sure, talented people excel all the time, but nowadays they do so in saturated markets. Everybody's got a book. Everybody's got a film. Print-on-demand and Youtube have democratized it all. To stand out in this environment, you can't just be good; you have to be a ferocious assault of excellence.

Now read *Balance* and tell me that it isn't one.

Then read all of Peter Giglio's work, and tell me that his grace isn't of the native kind.

I can't speak for everyone else, but when I see talent like this, I like to respond by talking about it. Wherever I can, to whomever I can. To ignore it would be as profane as looking away from a shooting star.

Don't look away. Look close. Look hard. A star is burning across the sky. You're entering into an encounter with Peter Giglio.

Consider this book introduced.

—Eric Shapiro/ Tarzana, CA/ 12 - 22 - 2011

This one's for the Shapiros—Eric, Rhoda, and Ben. Thank you for helping me find Balance.

CHAPTER

—1—

Geoff Singer was a sad man, never able to find balance in his lonely life. He was afflicted with a malady that drove people away: he tried too hard.

He hadn't always been that way.

As a child, he was labeled average. Not an underachiever. *Average.* No hope for greatness. No fear of failure. Living in the shadow of his delinquent brother, Ray, he'd done his best to cultivate that description; to fade into the wallpaper, unseen and unheard. Anonymity seemed the best approach not to disappoint his parents, whose time and worry were consumed by Ray. Their dissatisfaction was already the stuff of legend.

But as Geoff grew into his teenage years, loneliness gripped him. No one was drawn to dull. No one courted average. So he began to overcompensate, trying to break the chains of the façade he'd created. The result was disastrous. By emulating nothing, he'd become a nonentity.

And as hard as he tried to fit in, his movements were strained, false, received with a fierce degree of rejection. He wasn't merely ignored. He was actively avoided.

As a man, he'd learned to fit in, to appear confident. But his identity was caged, guarded. An even greater problem existed: he didn't know his true self, couldn't put it on display even if he wanted to, no matter how hard he tried. Something deep inside cried out for release, but he didn't know what that something was, or how to free it.

Now, alone on the veranda of The Grind House, he clutched a mug of coffee for warmth as he waited for her, the one he'd hoped would help him discover who he was. They had spent a lot of time here—chain-smoking her cigarettes, talking about anything and everything. Affectionate nights in warmer times, the café patio alive with chattering customers, alive with Amanda—her wide emerald eyes, long black hair, luminous smile.

Downtown Lincoln, lively on past Saturday nights in September, looked abandoned now. A patina of snow and ice glistened on empty streets, ashen flakes drifting earthward in yellow star-bursts of sodium vapor. It was like this everywhere, according to the news. Even though *Farmers' Almanac*—the weather bible for those in or near farming communities—predicted a mild season, winter had settled on the world three months prematurely.

But Geoff wasn't concerned with the weather. He was consumed by one despairing thought. She was leaving.

Amanda had broken the news two weeks earlier. It was last call at O'Rourke's, a pub they frequented after work. That wonderful night had slipped away too quickly, lost in cheerful banter and copious draughts of Guinness.

As he rose to get their final round, she rested a delicate but firm hand on his arm. "I need to tell you two things," she had said, struggling, he could tell, to sustain her smile. Her eyes narrowed like they did when she was angry—a rare state of being for her, and an emotion she'd never directed at him. Contrary to her expression, she'd said three words that stunned him. "I love you."

She'd been mad, he now ruminated, trying to block out the distant squeal of a vehicle's failing belt; mad for feeling what she had, maybe the way she still did. Anger was a bizarre sentiment to accompany love, but, in his experience, not a foreign agent.

His ex-wife had always refused to end a conversation without expressing her affection, even though most of their discourse was laced with contempt for him. "You let people walk all over you, Geoff," she'd said. "You have no verve, no core. No fight. I don't know what I ever saw in you, but...I love you." It seemed she needed to profess how she felt, or ought to feel, as a reminder. She had even said, "I love you," as she stood in the driveway, car packed, eyes filling with tears.

But Amanda hadn't cried when she said it. Her smile returned and her gaze widened as if a monumental weight had been hefted from her shoulders.

He'd been filled with hope as he settled back into his chair, taking her hands in his.

Fixing him with soul-piercing eyes, she'd said, "You won't like the next thing I have to tell you." Then she dropped the bomb. She was moving away, starting graduate studies in English at the University of Memphis, come spring.

Ten years younger than him, Amanda had graduated from The University of Nebraska the previous year, and then taken a job at Bradbury Research, where they had met. As her supervisor, he tried to establish professional boundaries, but the spark between them was strong—he could feel it; she said she could, too. So they started hanging out.

"When're you leaving?" he had asked.

"In two weeks."

"Why so soon?"

"I've never lived away from home, and...I need time to get settled before school starts. Please don't be mad at me, Geoff. Please."

He wasn't mad at her; not then, not now. He understood, at least he wanted to. She was young, afraid of commitment, and ready for new adventures in a bigger city. Unlike him, Amanda was impulsive and adventurous. He admired her.

Standing, he'd motioned for her to do the same, and then taken her in a tight embrace he never wanted to end. But it had ended, as all things do, and far too soon.

He kissed her on the forehead as she was getting into her car that night, and promised to visit her in Memphis.

"And, don't forget, we still have two weeks before I leave," she had said.

"Promise me we'll hang out a lot in those two weeks."

"I promise."

"You scared?"

"*Terrified*, but also excited...I just don't know what I'm going to do if things don't work out."

"You call me and I come get you. I'll take you anywhere you want to go. That's how it will go down."

"Do you promise?"

"I promise."

His cell phone, face down on the plastic table in front of him, vibrated. He and Amanda always kept their phones turned down when together, a practice she'd initiated. "I want to give you my full attention when I'm with you," she had said. The ritual was silly. It made more sense to turn ringers off or put phones away. But disagreeing with her, even on trivial matters, felt wrong. He hated himself for avoiding conflict, but was scared to push Amanda away. And yet, she was leaving anyway, just like his wife had.

He picked up the phone with a shivering hand and read the new text message.

Car won't start...sorry, can't make it. xoxo, Amanda

With numb, frantic fingers, he responded: *I can come get you, or we can chat on the phone?* He felt good about the message, counterintuitive to his instinct to respond: *Okay. Have a safe trip.*

"Sir, are you all right out here?" It was a waitress, bundled in a long winter coat, breathing white vapor, a concerned expression on her cherubic face.

"I'll be leaving soon," he muttered.

"Okay, but I'm going to have to ask you to come inside otherwise. It's below zero out here."

"I understand." He finished his coffee in one swallow and handed her the mug. A curt nod, and then he stood. "Thank you," he said in a thin, tired voice. His phone began vibrating again.

Amanda: *I wish we could get together for a proper chat, but I'm leaving early tomorrow morning and I'm dog-tired. Sorry! Love you, dude!*

"Dude?" he whispered.

"What?" the waitress asked, spinning on her heels as she opened the door of the café.

A burst of warm air greeted Geoff's frigid face. "Sorry," he said, "just mumbling to myself—hey, quick question, though. When a girl says 'Love you, *dude,*' what does she mean?"

"Is she your sister?"

"No. Why?"

"That's how I always tell my brother I love him."

"That bad, huh?"

The waitress, a nervous smile on her kind face, nodded.

Walking away from The Grind House, he pressed the TALK button, put the phone to his ear, and waited for Amanda to answer.

In a poll he'd compiled for Bradbury Research, an overwhelming number of participants between the ages of eighteen and twenty-six indicated a preference for text messaging versus talking on the phone, citing, as the primary reason, the greater sense of privacy and control it gave them. Amanda, twenty-four, was unrepentant of the same mindset. Four short rings and her voicemail picked up.

Unsure of what to say, he ended the call.

Would it have mattered, he asked himself, had he said

he loved her, too?

———

"Who're you texting?" Travis asked.

His eyes betrayed suspicion—an unbecoming trait she'd never glimpsed in him. *Now is not the time for doubt*, Amanda Herbert reminded herself, putting an arm around his tense shoulders. "No one," she said. One hand trailed across his arm as she placed the phone face down on her parents' coffee table. She turned back to him, eyes wide, smiling. "You have my full attention now."

Travis looked dubious, and she knew why. He was still upset about the secret she was keeping from her parents.

"Why can't we tell them?" he whispered.

"Because they won't let me go without a fight, and...I don't want that. What I want, more than anything in the world, is to leave with you. I love you."

It wasn't that her parents wouldn't let her go. After all, she was an adult, at least in terms of age. They would make things difficult and unbearable, though, wanting to discuss plans with her and Travis. Truth to tell, she didn't have a plan. Despite what she'd told Geoff, she wasn't enrolled in grad school; Travis was. Father would accuse her of acting impulsively, and Mother would assume she'd gone off her meds again, but she hadn't. *She wouldn't*. Waking in the ER, wrists bandaged, she'd learned not to tackle depression on her own terms. Maybe she *was* acting impulsively now, she thought, but for the right reason. She didn't want to lose Travis.

"Love you, too," he said, voice rising in volume. "But, Amanda, you're making me complicit in this. Think about it. They'll always look upon me with resentment. And, for the love of God, you're a grown—"

"Hush." She put a finger to his lips and in a low, thin voice murmured, "I don't want them to hear us."

She'd met Travis two months previously at a party. Far from being the best-looking guy in the world; but, there was something about him—the nervous way he smiled, the way he fidgeted in social settings. Confidence wasn't a virtue Amanda valued. She saw Geoff as confident, the kind of guy who could and would converse with anyone, regardless of shared interests. Travis was...*selective*, and far more injured. She was drawn to injury.

She could tell that her parents, sensing she and Travis were too much alike, didn't approve of him. Not that they didn't like him—her mother and father were very kind people. They just didn't trust him.

Her phone rattled against the glass surface of the coffee table.

"Aren't you going to get that?" he asked, annoyed.

She shook her head and then lunged at him. Open

mouth finding his, her hesitation found its way out the door to die in the freezing September night.

———

Bouncing up and down on a bean-bag chair, Shane Junior stared at a trio of gyrating puppets on the dirty screen of the console TV. Ginny Jenkins, a few feet away, changed her baby. Peeling back a disposable diaper, she was greeted by a solid, almost adult-looking turd. Her face lit up with pride. "Baby Gracie," she cooed. "You're growing up so fast, aren't ya?"

The show Shane Junior was watching came to an abrupt end, and he began to cry.

"Hold on, Junior," she pleaded.

His needful wailing didn't abate.

She wished television programming would return to normal so it wouldn't be necessary to play disc-jockey to an impatient two-year-old all day. Everything on TV was news now, and she didn't think Junior would like that much. Hell, she didn't care for it either—a bunch of talking heads rattling on about climate change and other things she couldn't wrap her own head around. And she was more than a bit miffed that she hadn't seen a new episode of *How I Met Your Mother* or *Two and a Half Men* in weeks.

Everything was about the weather now—the goddamn

weather. And damned-fool-Shane, a man she hardly recognized ever since his mother had died six months ago—not that she'd cared much for him when she could recognize him—was out there in it, at the West Plains Wal-Mart, picking up what he called "survival provisions." She silently prayed his truck would career off Arkansas-63 on his way back, killing him after a protracted period of lonely suffering. But then, seeing Shane's eyes and nose in Gracie's cherubic face, she hated herself for courting dark thoughts.

When she met Shane five years earlier, he'd been a deputy with the Fulton County Police Department. She and her family—she was sixteen at the time—had just moved from Kentucky, and she didn't know anyone in the area. Her older brother, Jason, introduced Shane as a hunting buddy and started to bring him around a lot.

Shane took an immediate shine to her. He seemed the sort she should be with, on the right side of the law and financially stable. Though she'd been underage at the time, her parents had approved of, even encouraged, the relationship. And so, three days after her seventeenth birthday, they'd been married in an outdoor ceremony, complete with a five shotgun salute and a pot-luck lunch.

Things hadn't been all bad. When he was around, which wasn't often, he was gentle with her. And he provided luxuries her family hadn't been able to—a house not on wheels, new furniture, and a car. But Shane was a man with many secrets.

She should've left him after the revelation he'd been abusing his authority, shaking down meth houses for cash. But, taking the advice of Tammy Wynette, she'd stood by her man through legal battles, promising the scared girl inside that she'd leave once the nightmare ended. But things only got worse. Following a final legal appeal, his firing from the police department made official, he'd seemed so sullen that she didn't have the heart to leave. A week later, she found out she was pregnant.

Now, she wrapped up another Huggie for the landfill and, with a grimace across her hardened-too-young face, crawled across the toy-strewn floor to the cluttered shelves of kid's movies. "Wanna watch *Barney*?" she asked, trying to sound cheerful. She had to snap her fingers twice to capture the toddler's roving attention. Gaze finally upon her, his cries reduced to sniffles, he gave a quick nod—more of a jerk—and reached out to her. She brushed a grape-jelly fingerprint off the front of the disc, and then placed it in the player. The room alive with everyone's favorite singing, purple dinosaur—*oh God, kill me now*—she returned to Gracie, pin-wheeling her chubby legs and smiling—always smiling.

And that made Ginny smile, too.

"Oh Gracie," she said, a tear running down her cheek. "What would I do without you?"

———

The pink panties Cassandra Parrish lifted from the laundry basket weren't hers. Even though she had no right to be mad—after all, *she* was the other woman—she was furious. Written in black marker on the garment's Fruit of the Loom label was EVE.

Despite her anger, Cass burst out laughing. What adult still labeled their underwear? Clearly, Joe's wife; no wonder he stepped out on her.

Dumping Joe's dirty clothes into the washing machine—he brought a load every two weeks when he passed through Springfield—she twirled Eve's panties on the middle finger of her free hand.

After starting the wash, she crept onto the patio of her mid-town apartment and lit a cigarette. Taking a deep drag, she scrutinized the garment, wishing it was stained with an embarrassing skid-mark. But no, Eve Plainview, little-miss-perfect-housewife—although she couldn't do her husband's wash properly—didn't even shit.

A wicked smile on her face, Cass lit the panties on fire with her Zippo, tossed it from the balcony, and watched it flutter like a dying bird into a snow-bank. With a shallow drag from her cigarette, she decided it was too cold outside.

Curling up on the couch next to her corpulent cat, Bono, she snatched a jigger, half-filled with gin and rapidly melting ice cubes, from the end table next to her. Draining the glass with one greedy gulp, she cringed as the piney liquid burned a trail from her throat to her stomach.

"Weeeeee," she squealed.

She chucked the glass across the room, watching, in mild horror tinged with drunken amusement, as it shattered against her framed *U2* poster from the band's 1992-93 *Zoo TV Tour.*

Startled, the cat leaped from her side with a judgmental hiss and scampered into the bedroom. Shards of gin-slicked glass ran down the singer's bug-eye sunglasses like slugs.

"Sorry, babies," she said, apologizing to both Bonos.

She started to cry. What had she become? She'd once been a professional writer, penning a trio of bestselling romance novels in the '90s. But her creative streak had long since shriveled up, as had the royalty checks from her defunct publisher. Nowadays, she spent her time working as a data-entry clerk for an insurance company—*mindless work for a mindless life.*

Her blurry gaze found a framed photograph, resting on

the end table. A kind child on the beach had snapped the image last year. Her eyes focused. California. She and Joe resting in the sand by the coastline of the big blue Pacific. The endlessness of the ocean and rekindled romance in her heart made her consider limitless possibilities on that hopeful day. She'd vowed that she would start writing again, and Joe, tenderly embracing her, had promised it was only a matter of time before he left Eve for her.

Looking back, the memory seemed much older than a year. And pledges made on that day rang hollow.

Two weeks ago had been her sister's wedding. The ceremony was beautiful, the altar bathed in flickering candlelight, shadows dancing across the faces of the bride and groom. Decked out in a stunning blue dress, standing as maid of honor, she'd wept through the duration of the ritual. Her sister, Lisa, had shot her a loving look that seemed to say, *"Someday this will be you."* In that moment, she hated Lisa—five years younger and happy. And *someday*, despite kind intentions, didn't feel like it would ever arrive.

"I love you, Joe," she cried, clutching the photograph to her chest. "More than anything in the world, I love you."

Then, mercifully, she drifted off to dream, as she always did, of Joe.

What the hell do I need with cages? Shane Jenkins asked himself.

But there they were. Three big-ass cages and he just had to have them. That's what Mother wanted. And what Mother wanted, *he* wanted.

A Wal-Mart employee, a smirk on his acne-ridden face, sidled up behind Shane. Mother eyed the interloper suspiciously; hell, she eyed everyone that way. But the kid looked all right—maybe a few quarts short of a full pan, but not a threat, even by Mother's cagey standards.

"Can I help you, sir?" the kid asked. According to the red-white-and-blue nametag on his vest, he was Casey.

"Yeah, Casey, you can start by telling me what the fuck these big cages are used for?"

Mother cringed. *"Language, Shane,"* she chided.

"Animals," Casey answered without hesitation. "Big dogs and such."

Looking at Mother, Shane said, "But we ain't got no dogs. Why, heck, you could fit people in cages big as these."

Smile widening, Mother nodded. The voice in the depths of his mind assured him she was right. He didn't understand—rarely did—but she was always right.

"Sir?" Casey asked in a bemused voice.

"Sold," Shane blurted. Reaching into his pocket for his wallet, he added, "Now, Casey, you think you can help me load these things into my truck?"

————

"I can't seem to find my pink panties anywhere." Eve moaned.

This is just like her. Joe Plainview heaved a sigh. The dumb bitch labeled and inventoried everything, as if all of her possessions were King Solomon's Treasure; the kind of woman who stuck a nametag inside every book she owned, including her three Cassandra Parrish novels.

Joe often found himself marveling at the spines of Cass's three volumes on Eve's cluttered bookshelves—not that he'd ever taken the time to read them, or any book for that matter. Life was a game to him. The game was a contact sport. And the name of one of his secret lovers repeated three times upon the mantle of his wife's material adoration was a trophy.

But the championship trophy, the thing he'd spent years restoring to better-than-original perfection, was the 1971 Pontiac Firebird in the garage. He loved the car more than anything or anyone in the world and would never dream of putting *his* name on her. She had her own name: Cherry.

A lot of his trucker friends listened to audio books to

pass the lonely nights on the road, but not Joe. He thought about Cherry—her glossy orange coat, the black racing stripes on her hood, the angry roar and alternately loving purr of her infallible 455—while he listened to Johnny Cash and Merle Haggard; he never got tired of the good shit those boys had laid down. When stopped for a break, he never felt like reading, although Eve and Cass routinely sent him away with books they promised he'd like. Hell no. He liked to fuck.

Certain his wife's precious panties were mixed up in Cass's laundry, he fixed his face with concern. "Ah, sweetie, I wouldn't worry about it. Were they the fancy kind from Victoria's Secret?"

"Well, no—"

"Then let's not worry too much, okay? I'll pick you up a few packs from the road."

"It's not that, it's...Well it's strange that something would just disappear—"

"Things vanish all the time, hon. I once left Michigan with eight pallets of Rice Krispies, and when I got them to Saint Louis, you know what happened? There were only seven of them on the truck; mystery was never solved. Thank God they weren't pallets of cigarettes and booze, or we'd be on the government tit right now." It wasn't exactly the truth. He'd left the eighth pallet in the Kellogg's

30

warehouse in Battle Creek and taken a serious reprimand for it, too. But the story fit nicely. He could really sling the bullshit when he needed to, which was almost always.

Eve smiled, smacking him playfully on the chest. "Oh, Joe, you and your stories from the road. You'll have to write a book about all your adventures one of these days."

Why? So you have another damn book to personalize with your infernal name like you *fucking wrote it?*

He smiled, taking her into his arms. "I believe I might just do that, sweetheart," he whispered into her ear.

Her fragile body wilted in his strong embrace. Lifting her lithe form, he took her to bed, Cherry's engine roaring through his mind.

—2—

If September came in like a lion, it left like a bomb.

Day and night, all over the world, snow and ice spat from gray, angry skies. Even Los Angeles, a city that hadn't seen snow since 1962, reported more than thirty inches by the middle of October.

Cities shut down.

In many places, power cut out.

Roads were impassable.

Airports closed indefinitely.

Every country declared a state of emergency. But not a single government was able to respond to the scope of the disaster.

The next Ice Age, the pundits declared.

The End of Days, proclaimed the blindly devout.

Politicians on the right argued with the left about climate change, mockingly insistent on calling it *global warming*—as in, "You call *this* global warming?"

And politicians on the left, not wanting to break with

routine, retreated without a fight.

But most people didn't care about the politics of weather. They were hungry, cold, and isolated. They wanted—*needed*—help. Those with electricity settled for the prosaic hum of television coverage. Those without power found religion.

Thanks to branding from around the clock cable news, the disaster became The October Blast; a name that, to many, sounded more gala-event-hosted-by-Dick-Clark than global calamity. But the name stuck, complete with 3D graphics and ominous music.

And with The Blast came a bug.

The Center for Disease Control, having neither the resources nor the required range of motion to track the source of the virus, could not isolate or classify the strain. So the infection became—again, thanks to cable news— The Blast Flu. The new flu was reported to be mild, only fatal to the aged or already unhealthy. The CDC advised the sick to stay as warm as possible, get plenty of rest, and drink plenty of fluids.

But, despite assurances, people—healthy people— began to drop dead like flies...

...and then they started to rise again...

———

October 30

Eyes glued to the computer screen, Amanda Herbert watched the brutal footage again.

From a carved-out path in Times Square, a reporter commented about the tall ridges of snow that towered above him. The camera panned up to show iconic billboards and buildings above a glacial trench, flakes twirling earthward.

Suddenly, the image became erratic. Crunching snow followed by a shrill, off-camera scream that crackled in Amanda's overworked speakers.

The image spun, destabilized. A sharp *thwack* as the camera met the ground.

However many times she'd watched the clip, Amanda's breathing quickened, her heart a sour snowball in her throat. From the other room, she could hear labored moans, perversely in synch with the video. Travis had a fever of one hundred and two, and with no way to get him to a hospital, she was terrified. Situation hopeless. What else could she do but watch?

A skyward Dutch angle framed the scene. What appeared to be a homeless man—filthy coat, icicles of hair pointing down from a red stocking cap—had clambered astride the cameraman. The homeless man, covered in snow, fought to maintain purchase on his quarry's bowed back. The cameraman flailed and wailed. And the reporter shrieked, pressed up against an icy wall.

The cameraman and his assailant collapsed to the ground, the image bobbing then stabilizing. Two faces, vagrant and victim, in frame, only the attacker...wasn't a *man*—eyes milky white, maw lined with serrated teeth, skin ashen gray...

A zombie!

The zombie bit deep into the man's neck and then yanked a bloody strand of flesh upward, exposing muscle and nerve endings. Blood spatter clouded the left side of the image as the gasping man was dragged out of frame.

The reporter frantically puffed white clouds, eyes closed. An arm cracked through the icy wall behind him, pulling him backward. Off balance, he slumped to the ground, screaming.

From outside the shot came sounds of the cameraman's fate—gnashing teeth, cracking bones, moist rending of flesh...

Breaking further through the tall ridge of snow and ice, the jutting arm became a short, dark woman in a lavender coat. The reporter, on the ground, raised his hands in front of his face. "No!" he pleaded.

The female zombie attacked...

Amanda's "Bohemian Rhapsody" ring-tone cut

through the tension, making her jump out of her seat. She stopped the video, snatched the phone from the desk, and took a deep breath, glancing at the display screen.

Incoming call...Geoff.

She hesitated, pressed TALK, sat down, and put the phone to her ear. Silence. Then, "Yes?" she muttered.

"Amanda?"

"Hi."

This wasn't the first time Geoff had called since she'd moved, but it was the first time she'd answered. She text messaged him occasionally to tell him how well things were going. But hearing the strained quality of her voice, she knew that veiling misery would be next to impossible now.

"Are you all right?"

His voice dripped with worry. He often slipped into a parental tone, as if the ten years between them were considerably more. But now—teetering on the precarious edge between independent bitch and damsel in distress—a budding part of her welcomed his worry.

"Amanda...you there?"

"Yeah, I'm...here."

"You all right?"

"Um...I'm alive...still."

"Well, that's good, I—"

"Look, Geoff—" A shadow grew across the carpet. She swiveled on her seat to see Travis, leaning in the doorway. Sweat beaded on his pale flesh like condensation on glass.

"I was just concerned about you," Geoff said. "You haven't been returning my calls."

Travis's bloodshot eyes narrowed. *Geoff*, he mouthed.

"This isn't a good time to talk," she muttered.

"Well, when is a—"

Ending the call, she met Travis's frosty glare with what she hoped were guiltless eyes. "Sweetheart, you look terrible."

"I *feel* terrible," he moaned. "Who's Geoff?"

"He's an old friend from work."

"Do you always hang up on friends?"

"Like I said, he's an *old* friend. I didn't feel much like talking to him."

"Then why'd you answer the goddamn phone?"

"I thought it might be...about my parents."

"Funny, I didn't hear you ask about them."

There was a threatening edge to his voice, almost predatory. Instinctively, she searched the room for a means of protection, fixed on the Louisville Slugger leaning against the inside wall of the room's cluttered closet, and prayed she wouldn't need it.

"You don't touch me anymore, *Amanda*. Do you know how that...*hurts* me?" Travis was crying now, fury dancing in his eyes.

"You're infected, sweetheart. I...I...do you want me to get sick, too?"

On trembling legs, he began his approach.

Don't let him touch you, the voice of self-preservation cried from the primordial depths of her brain. And even before the thought was finished, she'd dashed across the room. She snatched the Louisville Slugger from the closet and then, spinning to face Travis, cocked it back, choking up on the handle like her father had taught her as a child. "Stay away from me," she shouted.

"You fucking cunt."

"Just back up and...go back to bed. I don't want to hurt you, but—"

"You wanted me to get sick. You *made* me get sick." Anger had a new mate in his eyes: insanity. Lips quivering, he cracked a grim smile. "*You* did this to me."

He took a step toward her, and she responded with a step back. "Go to sleep, Travis. I want you...No! I *need* you to get well."

"But you know that *won't* happen."

He lunged at her.

Sidestepping his clumsy attack, she swung the bat at his

head. A dull crack. Wood connected with his temple. Head jerking askew, something snapping, he collapsed to the floor with a choked gasp, his body splayed like the chalk outline in a cheap murder mystery.

She didn't need to check his pulse. The stillness of his form told her he was dead.

————

The power had been out in Springfield for more than a week, and Joe and Cass knew nothing about reanimated corpses.

Shivering from fever and the growing chill of the room, Joe stared out the window of Cass's bedroom with vacant eyes. In the parking lot, obscured under a growing mountain of white, sat his cab-over Pete. The freight box had already been delivered three weeks ago to a destination a few blocks from Cass's place. At that time, he could have made it home—*should have gone home*—although the drive would have been treacherous, as it had been on his way into town. But Cass had convinced him to stay. And now the highway that led to West Plains was closed. So were all other routes out.

Huddled under a duvet and a pile of gaudy afghan blankets, she stirred. "What did you say, Joe?" she mumbled, rubbing sleep from her eyes.

"I didn't say anything."

She was a fool to keep sleeping with him. He was sick; had spent most of the night vomiting. But her love for him seemed to know no boundaries. He guessed he should be grateful; none of his other women were nearly as devoted as Cass, and, for the most part, he liked her. He even told her routinely that he loved her, although he wasn't sure it was exactly true. Still, he knew the words were important for her to hear, moreover they kept her around. After all, she was good where it counted, between the sheets, and he didn't want to lose his favorite fuck-buddy.

His mind drifting, he wondered how Eve was holding up. Not that he particularly cared. He'd tried to call her a couple times, to no avail. He imagined her at Wal-Mart or Target if the storm had finally abated there, spending more of his money on things to label with her name. Eve refused to carry a cell phone, having become convinced they caused cancer after watching a *60 Minutes* report years ago. So getting in touch with her was not always easy, even under the best of circumstances.

Cass was slowly rising. "Is it still snowing?"

A grim expression on his face, he nodded.

"When all of this clears up, we should go back to California," she said. "I had so much fun there last year. I even enjoyed the drive out, getting to see how you work."

He pulled his black Smith & Wesson 1911 from the

nightstand and, sitting on the edge of the bed, studied it. The gun normally rested in a hidden compartment beneath the driver's seat of his eighteen-wheeler, so he rarely had the opportunity to marvel at its sublime form—the vertical slashes across the slide that ran parallel to the handle, the perfectly designed grip with thumb guard. He loved the gun, but it was no replacement for Cherry; a sudden flash of the garage collapsed in on *her* sent a chill up his back. "Do you really think this will clear up?" he intoned.

A gentle hand on his shoulder, she said, "It has to, Joe. It just has to."

He sensed optimism in her voice, and it scared him. How could anyone be happy in the face of death? Cut off from the rest of the world. No TV. No radio, either, since Cass didn't stock batteries in the apartment. And there was no way to charge his phone, which had to be left off most of the time to preserve what juice remained in it. The few things they could eat—dried and canned goods—were running out fast. He didn't think it would take long before the building's pipes froze completely and water stopped running from the faucets.

"You finally cornered me," he said, shaking his head.

She laughed nervously. "That's ridiculous. Why would you—"

"We're going to die." He spun on her, eyes narrowing.

"Do you get that, Cass? We aren't playing house here. This...this apartment is our tomb, an icy fucking tomb." He grabbed her by the shoulders and shook her, his face reddening. "This doesn't end well—get that through your fucking head." He pointed at the window with a tremulous finger. "Look outside, see for yourself."

A lone tear slipped from her eye.

Heavy footfalls came from downstairs. In the distance, a woman screamed.

"Listen to that," he said. "People are already turning on each other. It's only a matter of time before—"

"At least we'll die together." She sobbed, clutching him as if he were a life preserver on a sinking ship.

He pulled away. "But I'm not ready to die, Cass. Not with you, not with anyone."

"We have to...make the best of things," she pleaded.

He shook his head.

Suddenly, there was pounding at the door.

Joe staggered into the living room. "What is it?" he bellowed, doing his best to sound threatening despite his weakened condition.

"Please, let me in," a young girl—a child—begged.

At Joe's back, Cass called out, "What is it, sweetie?"

"Do you know who it is?" Joe whispered.

"Sounds like Ruby Hernandez from downstairs. I

43

babysat her a few times."

"Now!" the girl pleaded. "She's coming after me."

Joe unlocked the deadbolt, pulled the door open, and Ruby rushed in.

Cowering by the base of the couch, the girl shouted, "Close the door!"

Gripping his gun, Joe stepped into the hallway. Dim, dust-filled rays of light bled through the blinds of a distant window. At the end of the corridor there stood a gray-haired woman in a dirty housedress.

"Sounded like someone was running through the hall," she said in a coarse, accusatory tone.

"You haven't been chasing after a child, have you?" Joe asked.

She shook her head, pointing down at his gun. "What the hell's the gun for? You haven't gone crazy or—"

Suddenly, an arm came around the corner of the hallway and wrapped around her throat. Another arm appeared, its hand splayed across the woman's temple. With a quick twist and snap, the old woman's body crumpled to the floor and began to twitch.

Her assailant emerged. It was another woman. Her head was angular to a freakish degree, and the way she moved was unnatural. She clumsily stepped over the dying woman and then began limping toward Joe.

"Who the fuck are you?" he barked.

"It's my mother," Ruby called out. "Please, shut the door."

Joe stole a glance into the apartment. Cass was cradling the terrified child. "You're burning up, sweetie," Cass soothed. "Don't worry, Joe and I will take good care of you."

Her mother. Joe shuddered. *What the hell is going on here?*

The woman was closer now, and he could see her features. She looked... No, it wasn't possible!

She looked dead.

Her eyes were pallid, glazed over as if consumed by cataracts, and her skin was an ashen, ghastly shade of pale.

"What the fuck?" He leveled his gun in her direction and took aim.

The woman—*the thing*—moaned, deep and feral.

"Stop or I'll shoot." He had often fantasized about using that line. But now that he had, there was no luster to the realized dream, only terror. His breathing quickened. Swirling spots appeared before his eyes.

The thing *didn't* stop. It advanced, arms held up and out as if in supplication.

Joe fired a warning shot above the woman's head. The report rang through the corridor, the scent of cordite clearing his sinuses.

She dropped to her knees, clutching her ears, screaming. Had he hit her? Leading with his gun, he approached cautiously; the thing shrieked insanely.

Cassandra bolted into the hallway. "Joe, what did you—" Catching sight of the horror show, she ran back into the apartment.

Joe leveled the barrel of the gun at the woman's head. "Start talking."

A malevolent screech came from her gaping maw, her rancid halitosis burning his eyes.

Joe squeezed the trigger, stumbling from the recoil. Her forehead erupted into bone and blood. She toppled backward, mouth open, eyes wide.

Like a bat out of hell, he raced back into the apartment as frantic footfalls echoed through the stairwell behind him, slammed the door, threw the dead-bolt, and slid down it, winded, his entire body slicked with sweat and his ears still ringing from gunshots.

Cass was holding the young girl and crying.

Joe got up and pushed a sideboard toward the doorway. "Help me, Cass." He moaned.

Cass laid the little one on the sofa and joined him in the effort. They only stopped when the hutch blocked the door.

"She's dead." Cass whimpered.

Joe steadied himself against a wall, tremors coursing through his body. "I know...I shot her."

"No...I mean Ruby. She's dead."

He glanced at the young girl and shrugged. He should have felt sorrow, he realized, but emotion was ebbing away, and he didn't have the strength to reach for it. His pulse was slowing. Spots multiplied rapidly in front of his eyes.

He fainted.

———

When the weather had started to take a turn for the apocalyptic, Geoff had calculated the distance between Lincoln and Memphis. Then, considering the MPG rating of his SUV, had figured he would need sixty-five gallons of gas for a two-way trip. So he'd purchased five fourteen-gallon portable gas-pumps, nearly wiping out his checking account. For filling the containers with gas, he had dipped into his savings.

A fierce wind rattled the garage-door against his back. He inspected the five red pumps, lined across the bed of his SUV, and prayed he would have a chance to use them.

Geoff routinely planned ahead. It was one of his obsessions. "You're forcing it," Ray would say. "Fantasizing fire when all you've got is ice." Blocking out Ray's voice, he focused on Amanda. She *would* need help.

And nothing, not even Armageddon, could keep him from her.

He slammed the hatch and went back into the house.

When he stepped inside, the phone was ringing. He snatched the cordless handset from the kitchen counter.

"Honey?" It was his mother in Omaha.

"Hey, Mom."

"How are you feeling? Not getting sick are you?"

"I'm fine, Mom. How about you?

"Fit as a fiddle."

"And Dad?"

"Same as he ever was. Geoff, I—"

"Look, Mom, can I...can I call you back later?"

"Yeah, sure, I just wanted to give you an update on Ray—"

"'Bye." Geoff hung up and heaved a sigh. The last thing he wanted to talk about was Ray, his convict brother.

Seconds later, the phone rang again. He hesitated a moment and then picked it up. "Mom, I'm busy right now."

"I can call back later if it's a bad time."

It was Amanda. And the sad tone of her voice cut straight to the quick, bringing tears to his eyes. "No...uh...I always have time for you."

"Dealing with your mother, huh?"

"Yeah, how'd you guess?"

Her laughter was weak and pained. He could tell she'd been crying. "Geoff, I...I'm a terrible person. I—"

"No you're not, Amanda. You're always your own worst critic, always—"

"Shut up, Geoff." There was an edge to her voice now. "For once stop projecting and just...just *listen*. My parents haven't answered the phone in days, and I'm freaking out, and...Geoff, are you still there?"

"Of course I am."

"There was strange static on my line, I'm sorry. I didn't tell them I was leaving, Geoff. I just...fuck...there's so much I need to..."

"Amanda?"

No response.

"*Amanda?*"

Dial tone.

Geoff dialed her number. After a single ring, he heard an operator three-tone: *Bu-du-boop. We're sorry, but the wireless number you have dialed is temporarily out of service. Please try again later.*

Without thinking, he grabbed his keys from a plastic rung on the side of the refrigerator, rushed to the garage, and pressed the button to lift the door. The overhead mechanism churned and whirred. But the door, frozen shut, didn't respond.

"Goddamn it!" His pulse raced.

Spurred by instinct, he got behind the wheel of his SUV. He started it and, fingers splayed across the steering wheel, revved the engine and then shifted into reverse. With a jarring crash, the bumper slammed into the garage door, the gas containers in the back sloshing and teetering. One container fell with a thud, releasing the pungent odor of gas...The door held.

He pulled the SUV forward, got out, and wrenched open the hatch. Gasoline spilled from the fallen container. He righted the pump, then found its cap and punched it back on.

The three windows of the garage-door that normally let light in were obscured by snow. What would he have done had the door opened? He didn't know. All he knew was that he needed to get to Amanda.

"She doesn't want you," Ray's voice sneered in his mind. "She'll use you, bro."

He dropped to his knees on the concrete floor. The impact was painful, but nowhere close to the ache in his heart.

———

Shane sat on the couch and stared at Mother.

"You know what'cher doing's the right thing."

He glanced down at the revolver in his lap, and a wave of sorrow enveloped him. Other than the steady whisper of the high-powered generator coming from the cellar, the house was eerily silent.

Ginny and the kids must be sleeping. And the thought of them—their pale, sickly faces—made him quiver with fear. Except for occasional cries from Gracie, they'd been sleeping for an unnaturally long time.

"Let them sleep. They'll be in the Dark One's grip soon, Shaney."

He looked up at her with moist eyes. "I can't do it," he muttered. "Not to Ginny and the kids." He opened the chamber of the revolver and stared at six copper butts. Hands trembling, he shook the bullets into his palm.

"Load the gun."

"No."

"Do it!" she snarled.

He shook his head; her shadow fell over him.

"Look at me," she said, her voice now calm and hypnotic.

Nervously, he met her eyes. "How can I do it?"

"The Lord has a plan for you, son. You are to become The Hunter."

"How am I supposed to do that? I'm too stupid—"

"Hush with that foolish talk. You'll cleanse the world of the

51

Scourge, and stand tall in the Kingdom of Heaven, a Righteous Warrior. I didn't raise no weakling now, did I?"

"No."

"Good. The Lord abhors weaklings."

"And then what?"

"Then you'll rule the new world, of course." She laughed.

"And what if I don't *want* to rule the new world?"

"You will. But first, let Mother help you." She sat beside him, placing a comforting hand on his shoulder. *"Everything's gonna be all right."* She leaned into him, her mouth stretching wide—*impossibly wide.*

Staring into the pitch black abyss of her maw, he froze. She came closer, until the darkness engulfed him.

The sensation of falling.

He closed his eyes.

And when he opened them, Mother was nowhere to be seen.

He was consumed by sadness. "Mama," he cried.

She didn't respond.

"*Mama!*" he shouted.

She had always been with him. Now he was on his own. He opened his hand and glanced down at the bullets. As much as he didn't want to do it, he knew what he had to do.

Mother was always right.

She was awakened by the sound of scratching. She looked up, her neck stiff but not pained, and saw a tree branch scraping against the eave outside the bedroom window. She heard crying and instinctively knew it was time for the baby's feeding. But her breasts, normally engorged with milk at a time like this, felt hollow.

She scanned the ceiling. Everything was in monochrome, like old movies only creepier. Shadows stood out in stark contrast to light, and everything fluttered unnaturally.

Hunger gnawed at her. She rose on one arm and saw the little boy—she couldn't remember his name—standing by the baby's crib. He seemed to leer through the bars in an unhealthy manner. The sight of him was disquieting, threatening. His mouth hung open and he grunted. *Little fucking animal.*

Her body sprang into action on its own. She pushed the boy aside violently, snatching her precious baby from the crib. She held the child, something within her screaming to feed, to feed on the baby...

No!

Battling the urge, she sat on the edge of the bed. Stroking the baby's head, she strove for the use of a gentle hand. But something told her, despite the struggle, she was handling the child far too hard. She tried to say, *"It's all right, Mommy's here."* But the only thing that came from her throat was a wet gurgle, making her aware that she wasn't breathing.

The baby cried louder, terror in its eyes.

In the corner of the room, the boy rose, eyes pale. As shadows, cast by the tree outside, danced across his features, he broke into a string of short, angry snorts. His intent was clear; he wanted her baby.

The door shot open, and a short, homely man with a bushy beard stood in the doorway.

Part of her wanted to scream, but she hissed at the man instead. Placing the baby on the bed behind her—*no, don't leave the baby alone*—she jerked upright, springing into an attack crouch. The man was food—she felt it deep within her core. Although she didn't understand, she sensed she didn't need to. She needed to eat—his flesh, blood, organs.

The man leveled a gun at her.

The baby's screams intensified. Momentarily in charge of her faculties—at least on some dim level—she glanced backward and saw the vile boy upon her infant. Like someone caught in a violent tug-of-war, her body flailed.

Tears streamed from the man's eyes, the gun trembling in his hands.

She sneered at him, hunger rising.

Gracie—*Yes, her name is Gracie!*—stopped screaming.

A bright blast of light.

Then, nothing.

————

His mind beginning to settle, a rational thought slapped him hard: e*mail!* Why hadn't he thought of it sooner? Assuming Amanda's power was still on, and she wasn't using dial-up or a DSL connection, it could be possible that she still had access to the Internet.

Geoff ran into his home office, opened the web browser on his PC, and logged into his email account.

And there it sat, like a gift on Christmas morning. One unread message from Amanda Herbert.

Time: 8:14 p.m. CDT
From: AHerbert@CompuNet.com
To: Geoff.Singer@bradburyresearch.com
Subject: (no subject)

Geoff - Power is cutting in and out so I'll be brief. Phones are dead; so's Travis. I'll explain later. Road conditions are impossible so don't kill yourself trying to get to me— please! But do check in on my parents—below are links for directions to their house and mine. My parents live in a two-story townhouse like yours. My place is unit B in an old house divided into apartments—brick with large white columns outside. I regret leaving. I love you, and I understand if you don't believe me. Love, A

He clicked *Reply*.

Amanda,

I LOVE YOU, TOO! I'll be there as soon as I can, and, of course, I'll check in on your parents ASAP. I hope this message finds you safely. I don't know or care who Travis was. Please know I'll come. Please wait for me. No matter what you do, HOLD ON TO HOPE!!

Love,
Geoff

He clicked *Send*, bolstered by validation. His preparations had not been in vain. "Fuck you, Ray," he shouted. "She loves me."

And now, sitting alone and waiting, as he'd done many times before, he didn't feel alone. He smiled. Amanda was waiting for him, too.

Two hours of hopeful anxiety ensued.

Then the power went out. The computer screen darkened save for a tiny luminescent spot in the center; a split second later that, too, disappeared.

———

October 31

Tears streaming down her face, Cass listened to *U2*'s "One" on her iPod to drown out the scratching and pounding at the door. She held Joe's head in her lap, stroking his long hair, staring down at his lidded, lifeless eyes.

One love...One blood...One life...

Unable to look at a dead child, she'd dragged Ruby's body into the hallway. Moving the china hutch on her own hadn't been an easy task, but she'd managed.

She knew it was Ruby at the door now, even though the child's voice had been reduced to grunts and growls.

If the child could cheat death, maybe Joe could, too.

She sang along to calm her raging mind. *"Carry each other..."*

She'd met Joe at a dive bar. It had been late, and she'd had too much to drink. A burly grunt in a John Deere hat and overalls had been harassing her for over an hour, leering at her with bloodshot eyes. He slipped his hand inside her shirt and smiled.

"No," she'd growled, slapping his hand away.

"Come on, baby. You write about romance; let's make a little romance of our own." His tongue shot out of his mouth, slithering across his chapped upper lip.

Earlier that night she'd talked to him politely, answering questions in only a mildly dismissive manner. He'd obviously taken it as a come-on.

When she'd gotten up to leave, the man responded by throwing his arms tightly around her waist, pulling her toward him. His face moved in on hers, his breath fetid. Strong, implacable arms tightened with such force that flashes of her dead body in a dumpster raced through her mind. Scanning the bar, she was terrified to find the place nearly empty. The bartender, her back turned to the scene, seemed to be in another world all together, yelling at someone through a cordless handset in her white-knuckled grip.

"One" had started playing on the jukebox.

And that's when it happened.

In her mind, the memory replayed in slow motion. A finger tapped the John Deere-guy's shoulder...He turned his head, a dumb expression on his sun-burnt face...A fist connected with his jaw...His eyes widened and his head rocked to the side, a tooth shooting from his mouth...He fell from his bar stool with a low, hollow groan, one hand raised skyward in a futile fist.

"Thank you," she had said.

The music swelled in the background.

"He didn't look like your type," Joe had responded in a calm, confident voice.

She met his gaze and was immediately entranced. His hair long but well groomed, smile wide and welcoming, eyes kind and understanding.

She collapsed into his arms without thought, fell in love without hesitation.

Now he was dead.

The song ended, and then started to repeat...

And Joe's eyes shot open.

———————

Shane was covered in blood, huddled inside one of his cages in the cellar. His body trembled, the family scrapbook splayed open at his feet. His fingertips left crimson streaks across Ginny's smiling visage.

He opened his mouth, jammed the barrel of the revolver into it, and cocked the gun. The taste of bloody metal made him wince and gag, his finger tightening on the trigger. This wasn't the first time he'd tried to do this. After he'd been fired from the police department, Ginny had found him in a similar state, ready to end it all.

"What the fuck?" she'd muttered.

He could tell she was scared. More scared than he was. "I'm nothing," he'd said. "I'm a worthless sack of shit."

"No. You made a mistake, that's all."

"I knew...what I was...doing. I wanted us to have nice things. I wanted you to...to respect me, love me."

She was silent.

"Can't even say you love me, can ya?"

"Shane, I...I've been meaning to tell you something for a couple of days now."

"You're leaving me, ain't ya? Been seeing it in your eyes for months now. You ain't gonna stop—"

"I'm pregnant."

That had made him want to stay alive then.

And it made him want to stay alive now.

He dropped the gun to the floor of the cage. "Mother never liked ya much, Ginny," he whispered, looking down at her face. "But you went and saved me. And if ya hadn't done it like ya did, I wouldn't be here now." He snatched her picture from the book and stuffed it in his mouth. Chewing the glossy paper was unpleasant, but, eventually, the photograph was soft, broken into manageable pieces.

He swallowed.

Electrical currents coursed through his muscles, making him stronger. His body steadied and his senses heightened. He smelled the truth at last; it was rancid, rotten, stale...*dead*. It wasn't what God had ordained for him. Not for His Special Warrior. Not for His precious world.

He crawled out of the cage, stood, and flexed his limbs. His lips curved upward as he studied the three side-by-side cages. A warped plan began to form in his mind. He wouldn't simply wipe out the scourge; he would make the sinners suffer.

"You was always right, Mama," he said. "Maybe you wasn't right 'bout Ginny. But you was always so smart when it come to me."

He picked up the family album, flipped through it until

he found a picture of Mother. He carefully pulled her image from the page, brought it to his lips, and kissed it.

He had Ginny to thank for his life.

And Mother to thank for his purpose.

He was changing.

———

The orange prescription vial was empty.

Amanda could feel her heartbeat.

Wrapped in a comforter and huddled on a recliner, she tried to stop the room from spinning. Closing her eyes would only make the world feel more out of control, and she couldn't close them, not even had she wanted to.

Eyes intent on the hallway, she was waiting for Travis.

Beneath the comforter, she clutched a cold, iron fire-poker. The fireplace, a thing which brought serenity in better times, blazed and crackled with a haunting, foreboding quality.

Her mind drifted.

Amanda had always been a loner. Even in high school, she'd possessed a dark, brooding quality that repelled others. She craved acceptance, but hadn't known how to achieve it. Painting her face with dark makeup, wearing black, even though she had no aspirations of being Goth, had seemed a way to gain attention. And it had, but not in a good way. The Catholic school she attended was preppy and elitist, and Amanda quickly went from being ignored to becoming the target of ridicule. In defiance, she grew more transgressive with her attire. Her parents begrudgingly agreed to nose and eyebrow piercings; the school subsequently banned them. She'd pleaded with her parents to let her attend public school, but they refused, insisting she see a psychiatrist.

Alone in her bedroom at night, listening to depressing music, rolling razor blades in her palms, she was certain she was not meant for the world she'd been born into. Perhaps her parents were right, she'd thought. Despite the pain of being, she didn't want to die.

Dr. Walsh, the psychiatrist, was not a nice person. According to him, everything was Amanda's fault. When she started the medication, it wasn't because of the doctor's prescription; it was because it placated Mom and Dad.

But when her mood actually started to lift, she was stunned.

Three weeks after popping her first pink pill, she met a guy named Mark Farthing. He attended public school and seemed nice. Too nice. He was, she told herself, way too good for her. He played football and his parents had money; he even had his own car. The new light in her eyes, she'd rationalized, attracted him to her. Convinced she'd finally found acceptance, she fell quickly into bed with him.

Sweet sixteen: his groping hands reaching into places only she'd known; hungry desire in his eyes; the warmth of his frantic kisses, passion she'd never dreamed of.

The aftermath: the light leaving his eyes, unreturned calls, isolation.

Certain the medication had defectively enhanced her state of mind, she'd flushed the remainder of the pink tablets from the orange prescription vial down the toilet.

The days that had followed were excruciating past reason.

One night, she drew a hot bath, laid two fresh razors on the edge of the tub, and climbed in.

The next thing she remembered was waking up in the hospital. Somehow her mind had blocked out the cutting moments. Small mercy; she'd always possessed the ability to suppress the most gruesome events of her life.

Now, expecting Travis to emerge from the hallway any second, she didn't know how she was supposed to cope with the situation. She had matured very little in the last eight years. Until a few weeks ago she'd still lived with her parents. She had less than ten dollars in her checking account—not that money had value anymore.

She was a loser.

But winning meant trying, and, even though her youth had been painful, she fought against adulthood with fierce intensity; if she conformed to the ways of the world entirely, she reasoned, she would become part of the same organism that had failed her.

There was a sudden crack overhead, then the sound of rushing water. She stood, looked out the window—the fire-poker still tight in her grip—and saw water dripping from the eaves of the old house. There was a bright clearing in the gray sky; through the widening gap, rays of light found earth. She pressed her hand against the dirty window pane, and hope seized her.

The glass was warm.

―――――

With unnatural suddenness, temperatures started to climb.

But power and the phone service did not return. Those with access to battery-powered televisions, radios, and laptops couldn't locate signals. Roads were slushy rivers of melting snow and ice.

The Blast was over...

And so, it seemed, was the world it had blasted.

Road crews didn't spring into action to clear streets and highways. Utility crews didn't climb poles to restore services. Elected officials didn't give inspiring speeches about perseverance and rebuilding.

Survivors crept out of their homes into the alien warmth of a new world...

And they were greeted by the dead.

———

The front door was open.

"Hello?" Geoff called out.

No response.

He crept into the home where Amanda had lived. Nothing fancy; living room and kitchen downstairs, bedrooms upstairs—just like his house. But the place was in chaos—chairs and books strewn about the floor, furniture toppled, and shelves emptied. There were torn couch cushions and bloody handprints on deeply scratched walls. And a nauseating, butcher shop odor permeated the air.

On the mantelpiece was a family photograph in a crystal frame. Amanda's mother and father were smiling. Amanda—twelve or thirteen in the photo—was the picture of misery—her mouth turned down, her eyes filled with despair. Geoff understood now why Amanda rarely talked about her childhood. He'd always considered her independent, self-assured, and always tried—*tried too hard*—to act the part he thought she wanted him to play. But now, he realized, she was injured. To think of all the time he'd spent with her, assuming he really knew her. In an instant, a cheap family portrait shattered all his illusions. If he'd fought for her sooner, she might be with him now. And he wouldn't have to be here.

He parted drapes that hung in front of a sliding glass door and then gasped at the scene in the backyard. Amanda's parents were crouched over a corpse—man or woman, he couldn't tell. Amanda's father gnawed on an arm while Mrs. Herbert greedily pulled organs and entrails from the body's gaping torso, her mouth a malevolent rictus. Her jagged teeth sank into what looked like a liver. She took a bite, then, swallowing without chewing, she tore off another chunk, her dark lips coated in viscera.

Geoff retched, staggered by a wave of dizziness. His mind screamed, *Run!* Yet, frozen by fear or steadied by purpose—he didn't know which—he continued to watch.

Mr. and Mrs. Herbert were both awash in blood. Their flesh, dark and beginning to separate, was more decomposed than the zombies he'd seen on TV. The lower half of Mr. Herbert's jaw was exposed bone, and Amanda's mother had only one eye.

Suddenly, milky eye narrowing, she howled so loud it sounded like she was in the room with Geoff. Dropping a strand of intestines, she stood—and looked straight at him.

Geoff rushed out the front door toward his vehicle. Wet footfalls followed him, and then came the clatter of a metal gate swinging against a post.

He scrambled into his SUV.

He couldn't breathe.

He scanned his door panel for the all-lock button, but his mind was frayed and he couldn't make sense of the controls—

A loud *crunch-thump*, then the sound of crumpling metal—

He gasped. Mrs. Herbert was on the hood, her drooling mouth hanging open, her gums and tongue the color of well-done steak. She clawed frantically at the windshield, her nails leaving trails of blood across the glass.

There was the sound of pounding to his right.

He turned his head—swimmy, disconnected—and saw Mr. Herbert, beating against the window with open palms.

Geoff started the car, shifted into reverse, and floored the accelerator.

The passenger window shattered, and Mrs. Herbert simultaneously slid from the hood, a startled look on her rotten face. The SUV dipped into the river-like road with a splash, and Geoff shifted into drive. Gas sloshing, containers teetering, he slammed his foot into the accelerator again. Arcs of water flew high on both sides of the vehicle.

He glanced right. Mr. Herbert's arm was wrapped

around the door frame, his blackened fingers digging into the armrest.

Instinctively, Geoff steered slightly right, grazing a parked car. A dull *thump*, the crack and chime of the sideview mirror shattering, and then the brief shriek of metal on metal. Once past the parked car he'd hit, he glanced at the rearview mirror.

Mr. Herbert was face down in muck.

Geoff jammed his foot into the brake, bracing himself against the jerk. He did a quick inventory of the gas containers, all upright, and then watched as Amanda's father rose.

Good, I don't have to tell Amanda I killed one of her parents.

With a quick left on 27th Street and then a right onto Nebraska-Highway 2, Geoff sped toward the girl he loved, the sun a sliver on the cloudless western horizon.

———

Amanda was jolted awake by the sound of her own cries. She grabbed the fire-poker from her lap and then crept cautiously into the hallway, hating herself for having fallen asleep.

Glancing into the computer room, she saw Travis splayed across the floor. Approaching him slowly, she noticed something new, a large, blood-coated hole in his forehead. She lifted the fire-poker and found its tip covered in blood, as were her sweatshirt and jeans.

The room began to spin, and the dream she'd been having came back to her. She'd stabbed Travis's head with the implement, but...*that had only been a dream. Hadn't it?*

Shadows danced across the room. She sensed someone—*or something?*—behind her and felt a poke sensation in the small of her back. She spun around, stabbing the air with the fire-poker.

Nothing there.

It's only my mind playing tricks.

She looked out the window. The sun was bright, the sky clear, and she was dripping with sweat. Did she have a fever? No. It was hot now. The streets looked like rivers, the yards like swamps.

Suddenly, someone stepped in front of the window outside. It was Mark Farthing—*but how?*—exactly the way she remembered him: varsity letter jacket, winning smile, shaggy brown hair.

"Aregghaaar," Mark said.

This was a dream. *It must be.*

"Eeerigghuh," he said.

She felt something touch her face and brushed it away. Her face was sticky—with blood. There was a stinging pain on her cheek, and she knew the blood was hers. She realized she no longer held the fire-poker, and that her clothes were no longer bloody. *How?* She looked back at the window. Mark was gone. Travis was gone, too. *How?*

She caught a whiff of something rancid—the scent of death and decay—and the smell seemed to be closing in, getting stronger. She felt a touch on her shoulder. She screamed…

… and her eyes shot open.

This time it *was* real. She was lying on the floor, and kneeling above her was Travis, his eyes pallid and his skin ashen gray. From the front window in the living room, the moon cast an unearthly pall upon his face.

"Arrigggghah," he wailed.

She rolled away from him, her eyes frantically searching for the fire-poker in the relative darkness. The sticky, warm pain still gnawed at her cheek.

"Fuck you, Travis," she muttered. And then in an angrier tone she said, "You scratched me."

Travis backed away, holding his hands out in front of him.

Her gaze landed on the fire-poker by the recliner. She scurried to it, snatched it with her right hand, gripped it tight, and rose on unsteady legs. "You fucking scratched me," she shouted.

Standing a foot away from him, her eyes narrowed.

"Arreggharr?"

She held the fire-poker up like a javelin and, with a sense of déjà vu, rammed it into his head with all her might.

He fell backward onto the floor, the make-shift spear protruding obscenely from his skull. His limbs flailed as he groaned and wailed.

Planting a foot into his throat, she grabbed the handle of the fire-poker with both hands. Leaning into the poker, she forced it down with her weight. There was a dull crack as the implement cleared Travis's skull then dropped effortlessly through his brain.

Tears rushed down her cheeks. "You fucking scratched me."

But Travis couldn't hear. He was gone.

———

Bleeding out on the couch, Cassandra watched Joe eat Bono. The sight made her cringe, but if it kept him from devouring her before she died, she was fine with that. She wanted to be whole when she came back, so she could be with him again—*forever.*

When he'd awakened in her arms, his face had moved languidly toward hers. She'd hoped he was going to kiss her but hadn't been at all surprised when he bit into her neck, wrenching away a large chunk of flesh with his teeth.

She'd screamed, intense pain burning a trail from her

neck to her back. Managing to break free, she'd scrambled into the bedroom where Bono was sleeping on the bed.

Offering the cat to him wasn't easy; he'd been her only companion on many lonely, sleepless nights. As Joe had taken the cat from her hands, anger and fear erupted in Bono's eyes. He hissed and flailed with admirable determination.

No use worrying about that now, the cat was dead, the deed was done.

Blood poured from her neck in a steady flow, and she could feel life ebbing away. Pain also faded; there was mercy in that. It was only a matter of time now.

She closed her eyes and thought of Joe.

Smiling, she died.

———

Just short of Kansas City on I-29, Geoff's radio, set to scan, fell upon a weak signal. He turned the volume up, caught some words among the static.

...edge of Platte City, our encampment...nineteen people...hear this, please join us...heading out...St. Louis in the morning...we... outnumber the dead...repeat, we currently outnumber...area has been hit hard. But in St. Louis...FEMA relief teams...electricity and clean water...safe zone...

Geoff's speakers filled with static. He briefly considered exiting the highway and turning around to rejoin the broadcast, but he thought better of it.

He had a plan. He would take Amanda to St. Louis.

Wind howled through the broken window, and it was good, imbuing him with an alertness he needed. He'd not seen other vehicles on the road. But, at the speed he was traveling, caution was prudent. He'd driven over a few bodies, animal and human, and steered around others he'd seen in time. He'd encountered flood plains too deep to navigate and had been forced to find alternate routes back to the highway with a Rand McNally road atlas (the GPS no longer functioned). Fog was so thick in places that he was only able to see a few yards in front of the high beams.

Merging onto 435-East at a speed of one hundred miles per hour, he allowed his mind to wander back to the first time he'd met Amanda. She was a new employee at Bradbury, and it was the last day of training, the day when new employees met their supervisor for the first time.

Speaking to the group, pacing around the front of the training room as he often did, he'd noticed her gaze, following him wherever he moved. Others showed the same signs of boredom he'd seen in hundreds of new employees.

"Come on everyone," he'd cajoled them. "I feel like I'm bearing witness to a zombie apocalypse here." That had earned him a few laughs, but not hers. Instead, she cracked a winning grin that seemed to say, *I'm yours*. Then, chin rested in upturned palms, she leaned forward, eyes piercing him with greater intensity.

After class was over, she approached. "I'm Amanda."

"Yeah, I know, you're gonna be on my team."

She wasn't great looking, not in the traditional sense, but there was a special quality about her, something he couldn't put his finger on. Was it that she paid attention to him? No, he didn't think so. It was an immediate sense she was a kindred spirit; it was in her eyes, indefinable.

"Do you like zombie movies?" she had asked.

"Yeah, I do. I like horror movies in general; have over a thousand of them in my collection at home."

"Awesome. That why you made the joke about zombies?"

"No. Funny story, actually. I compiled a research study two months ago where we surveyed two thousand people between the ages of twenty and twenty-nine. We asked them what their greatest fear was. Twenty-six percent of them said it was a zombie apocalypse."

She'd laughed. "They were pulling your leg."

"Oh, I don't know. That would mean over five hundred people were pulling our legs. That sounds more like a conspiracy than a joke. The good news is the client we compiled the research for is a Hollywood studio, so if you like zombie movies you're bound to get more."

"How old are you?"

"Thirty-three."

"That's why you don't understand."

He'd laughed. "Maybe. Or maybe it's why I do understand."

"I like you, Geoff."

"Yeah, I like you, too, Amanda."

"I normally don't like people. I just wanted to put that out there."

"Then...I feel special."

"You are. But don't let your head swell."

"Thanks."

"See you around."

"Whether you want to or not."

And now, he wondered if there was any significance to the poll. Twenty-six percent: more than global climate change, more than terrorism, more than the struggling economy. It hadn't seemed right to him then and it seemed even weirder now.

Mankind has been polluting the earth for years. Is the earth...claiming payback? Is that the right word? Can a planet be sentient?

He didn't know. But he knew The October Blast hadn't been a new Ice Age. He knew that Ice Ages lasted a lot longer than a month, and the temperature gauge on his dashboard read eighty-nine degrees.

No. Something else was going on. Zombies weren't exactly natural. But did that mean they weren't part of nature's plan?

Fuck, did the planet read the minds of youth? Or did youth read the mind of the planet?

Alongside the highway, a long procession shambled. As he sped past, their heads turned to scrutinize him, their argentine eyes like highway reflectors in the high beams. A thick wall of fog began to roll in, but he maintained his speed, not wanting to give a zombie the chance to lunge through the shattered passenger window.

No matter what they have in mind, zombies won't be polluting the planet anytime soon.

Suddenly, his theory didn't seem so crazy.

———

He would let her become.

He picked meat off the cat's hind leg and slowly chewed it to keep his vision clear and colored, and the beast within from taking control.

He would let her become, not because he loved her, but because he would need her. She was dead on the couch now, but she would be back soon. She wouldn't take long; she never kept him waiting. She would become, and then they could leave.

And he would *let* her become. He needed a shield if bullets started to fly; he needed someone to watch his back when he couldn't; someone to jump in front of things to save him without a moment's hesitation. He could *let* her do that.

Bottom line: he had to get to Cherry. And then, once he and Cherry were reunited, all bets were off. The couch-corpse, or whatever her fucking name was, could do whatever she liked if she hadn't been destroyed by then.

But for now, he would be patient.

Outside, breathers were walking and talking; he could hear them through the screen door of the patio. They were scared. And scared people meant guns. He pulled the gun out of his jeans and held it in front of his face. His digits were not as cooperative as they used to be, but after some struggle, the handle was in his grip, his finger tightening on the trigger.

He wasn't like the others of his kind; he was a breed apart; he had a gun, too.

Her eyes shot open.

Hot damn! Time to roll!

———

His movements were sublime. The way he listened before turning a corner; the way he crept even though his body was stiff; the way he led her by the hand into the safety of shadows.

Wisps of mist rose from the moist ground like smoke-serpents, making the air dense, and her flesh wet. In the distance, two breathers heaved bodies of her kind into a dumpster.

He motioned for her to hang back; her low growl uncontrollable, she knew he couldn't risk detection by having her join the kill. She needed to feed, hunger burning deep. But she was sure he would provide.

He snuck behind a tree next to the dumpster, the shadow of his form flickering in the fog-drenched moonlight.

"Do you think there are more around here?" asked one breather.

"I don't know," said the other. "They might be slow and stupid, but we still have to be careful. We need to—"

A blast from his gun dropped one of them to the ground. The other knelt by his companion's side, crying.

She covered her ears and closed her eyes, the echo of the gunshot ringing through her head. She could hear her lover wail and knew the blast was affecting him the same way. When she opened her eyes, her lover's gun was leveled at the crying man's head. She steadied herself for another shot and then it came. Sonic waves of head-splitting torture made her shriek in agony.

A pained look on his face, he motioned for her to approach.

It was dinnertime.

As they fed, she could feel her body calming, and the echoes of gunshots receding. The shadows of the night faded away; the world became bright and colorful. Happy in that moment, she sensed her *someday* had finally arrived.

She smiled at him.

He sneered.

Her happiness was marred by gloom. The night still burned bright, but she wasn't part of it. She was disposable, the other woman.

After a while, they loaded meat into the cab of his truck. He supervised her movements with grunts and growls. She complied with every command.

Soon she was sitting next to him in the truck, gnawing on a dismembered arm while he figured out the controls. One of his hands was splayed awkwardly on the steering wheel, the other on the shifter. The grinding of gears told her that he was having trouble, but she continued to chew contentedly, not expressing frustration.

Finally, he managed to get them out of the parking lot and after a few wrong turns, onto the highway.

He had a hard time maintaining control of the truck,

and their progress was slow. But she knew he would get them wherever they were going. She hoped it would be California, but couldn't for the life of her remember why.

————

It was clear to Tyson and Drew that Darrell was their leader. More than ten years older than them, Darrell had seen a lot and knew more about the world than they did.

"Boys," Darrell said, "what we've got here's a situation."

They listened intently, sensing this was a bad time to interrupt. Darrell was unpredictable, prone to fits of rage given the slightest—often imagined—provocation.

"Drew, you still got them road flares?"

Drew nodded.

Darrell snatched his shotgun from atop a stack of *Soldier of Fortune* magazines and cradled it against his barrel chest.

"What you got in mind?" Tyson asked.

Drew shot Tyson a fearful glance, mouthing the words, *Shut up.*

"Ain't I got the right to—" Tyson started.

"Shut the fuck up," Darrell bellowed, "both of you." He stood, most of his face obscured by shadows. But, in dim light from the lantern, they could make out a thin sliver of a smile.

An evil smile, Drew thought.

"You boys have seen *Mad Max*, right?"

They nodded.

"Well, what we've got is a real *Mad Max* kinda situation on our hands. Problem is, we ain't got no gas, and we ain't got no pussy."

"Don't recall Max doing much fucking," Tyson said.

Drew slapped Tyson across the back of the head, pointing at Darrell with his free hand. "Listen," he whispered.

"Boys, what I got in mind is a little road block. We got guns. We got survival instincts. And it's high time we had a little fun. World's gone to shit, and if we don't take a stand, we might as well wait for the creepers to come and get us. Drew, how many creepers you take down today?"

Drew held up six fingers.

"How 'bout you Tyson?"

"Two."

"We're already kickin' ass for the good of Mankind, and all we got to show for it is a pile of rottin' creepers, some dirty-ass water, and big, swinging dicks with nothin' to stick 'em in. We're in charge now." Darrell pumped his shotgun. "Who's with me?"

Tyson and Drew were too scared to cop out. As much as they hated to admit it, streetwise Darrell had kept them alive. He knew how to hunt. He knew how to survive. They'd be lost without him.

Drew ran to his trailer and grabbed his road flares.

Tyson salvaged a few boards from behind Darrell's house and, using tar for paint, fashioned a crude sign.

Within an hour of Darrell's idea, they'd staked out a spot on Missouri-60.

"Drew," Darrell said, "you watch the woods for creepers. Tyson...You *listening* boy?"

Tyson was planting his sign into the soft shoulder of the road. "What?"

"Boy, that sign looks about as ugly as your mama on Easter Sunday."

Tyson, the one who'd shot his mother in the head when she turned, looked like he might cry.

"You've got road duty," Darrell said.

"What's road duty?"

"Stand in the middle of the road and wave your gun, get assholes to stop and such. Think you can handle that?"

Two headlights were cutting a swathe through the fog. Tyson stepped into the road.

"Now aim your gun at them," Darrell said.

Tyson could tell that it was a large truck, moving in serpentine patterns. He leveled his handgun, his arms trembling with fear. "They're all over the place," he muttered.

"You're doing fine, boy," Darrell shouted.

"Don't you think we should put the flares down first? Fog's getting thick," Drew said.

"You gonna keep an eye on the woods or second guess me all night?" Darrell snapped.

Tyson aimed into the air and fired. But the truck didn't slow. Silver beams sliced through the haze, sweeping the night. He leveled his gun and shot at the grille of the truck. Sparks arced from metal. But the truck didn't slow.

"Put one through the windshield, Tyson," Darrell bellowed. "They'll stop for you then."

Tyson aimed for the windshield, squeezed the trigger, and missed. The truck was close now. In the moonlit mist, he glimpsed the driver and froze with fear. The ghostly visage behind the wheel could be only one thing.

"Zombie," he muttered.

"What the fuck?" boomed Darrell.

"*Zombie,*" Tyson shouted. Summoning the strength to move, he started for the shoulder but was too late. He was splotched to the front of the truck, where most of his mangled corpse would adhere for another twenty miles.

———

The very air was burnt.

He pulled into the long driveway that led to the house,

his hackles rising. Tall trees lining the winding trail were scorched and blackened. As his house came into view in the high beams, he emitted a low, fearful groan. The house, like the trees, was charred. The roof was gone, as was much of the structure...including the garage.

He stopped the rig, climbed out, and slogged to the space where the garage had stood. There, amongst the detritus of his house, he found Cherry: black, blistered, dead.

He threw his head back and howled into the night, his hand caressing her rough, wounded body. Etched in ash on her back window was a perplexing message: *EVE*. Peering through the space in the *V*, he glimpsed a blackened skeleton that seemed to be curled up in the backseat.

Something touched his shoulder. He spun and saw the couch-corpse trying to smile ingratiatingly and look pretty, but her face was disgusting. She needed to back off if she didn't want to get hurt. There was no way she could understand what he was going through. How could she? She was only a woman. He turned his back on her and started blindly toward the woods. He knew he needed to get away, yet couldn't abide the thought of driving the truck another mile. Grinding gears and the roar of an inferior engine were too much pain to handle. He wasn't the driver he used to be, but Cherry would have taken care of that for him. Unlike the eighteen-wheeler, Cherry did her share of the work when it came to the open road.

Squelching footfalls behind him told him that the couch-corpse was following. *Dumb bitch.* He couldn't stop her. If she wanted to follow, fuck it, he would let her. He might still need her anyway.

He stopped. Reaching down the front of his pants, he grabbed his tiny and flaccid penis. Despite the stench from his shit-filled pants, he stroked his cock. He tried to focus his mind on erotic images, but his manhood didn't respond. It was dead. He pulled the gun from his belt and tried to grip it, but that was useless, too. His fingers had stiffened and wouldn't wrap around the handle. He grunted. Fingers stiff, cock limp, Cherry burnt to a crisp— he was in hell. As much as it pained him to realize it, he wasn't a breed apart. He was one of them now, one of the shambling masses, driven by insatiable hunger.

The couch-corpse moaned. The exposed muscle and nerve endings of her neck looked like road-kill in the moonlight. *No wonder I can't get a boner.* He tried to laugh, but all he managed was a high-pitched shriek. That was okay, humor was far from what he wanted to express.

He was hungry again, despite his recent feeding. His body ached and his head screamed. He regretted not stopping to eat the three men that had shot at the grille of his cab-over, although running one of them down had been fun. The bones from the dumpster kill had been picked clean. New flesh was needed. The couch-corpse had been dead too long to eat, which was a shame; it would have been nice to kill two birds with one stone.

Glancing at the trees around him, the space between them murky with fog, he remembered the wilderness had been filled with life. What kind of life, he couldn't remember. But instinct told him it was the right place to hunt.

CHAPTER

—3—

November 1

The house was surrounded, her blood infected. Shadows played across the bathroom floor, footfalls swished outside. It was only a matter of time before they made it in; a matter of time before they discovered her flesh.

At least if they eat me, it may keep me from coming back as one of them.

Amanda sent a heartfelt thought to Geoff through the ether: *I'm sorry. Please don't come for me. Save yourself. I love you.*

The water was cold. Her life spilled out in clouds of darkness from the deep slashes in her wrists. The thought of being eaten alive terrified her more than the possibility of reanimation.

This was her way out; her only way...

———

"Out!" the redneck demanded. "Get the fuck outta the car now, or I'm gonna blow your fuckin' head off."

A line of road flares cut through the shadowy night,

illuminating a crude, hand-painted sign that read, ZOMBIE CHECKPOINT. One redneck eyed the gas containers in the back while the one at Geoff's passenger-side window, a big mother-fucker, held a shotgun across his chest. Glaring contemptuously at Geoff, the oaf's face was pink in the unearthly glow of the flares. "Are you listening to me?"

"I told you," Geoff said. "I'm not a zombie, I'm not infected, and—"

"We'll be the judges of that, boy," the skinny redneck, much younger than his companion, called out from the back of Geoff's SUV.

"What gives you the authority to do this?" Geoff asked.

The hefty redneck laughed. "Authority? There ain't no more fuckin' authority in the world." Aiming the shotgun at Geoff, he bellowed, "Now get out. We've already had enough trouble for one night, and we ain't looking for no more."

Geoff held up his hands. "Okay," he said in a calm, defeated voice. "Give me just a—"

"*Now!*" screamed the man with the gun.

"Have him unlatch the back," said the young redneck.

The monster turned to his partner, a look of contempt on his face, and—

Geoff jammed his foot on the accelerator, clutching the

wheel, his knuckles white. The back passenger side window exploded in a thunderous blast and a spray of glass. He steered around a flare, breath and pulse a rataplan of chaos in his head. Another shot rang out; a dull, harmless sounding *zing* from the back bumper.

Watching the line of flares shrink in his rearview mirror, he inspected his body for wounds. Albeit showered in pebbles of glass, he wasn't hit. He breathed a sigh of relief and felt a semblance of normalcy—like he might not die of a heart attack at any second—return.

Rural Missouri hadn't been a fun place to travel when the world was alive; go figure now. No more stops, even if the fuckers *were* brandishing guns. The remainder of his trip would cover areas with low-population density, meaning less chance of zombie contact. Redneck nut-jobs he wasn't as sure about. Wondering which was worse, he couldn't land on a definite answer. He only knew one thing—

"I'm coming, Amanda!" he shouted, a determined smile widening across his face.

———

"Fuck," Darrell shouted. "Can't you do anything right?"

Drew hung his head, wanting to say something to defend himself, but he didn't have the courage. When he glanced up, fighting back tears, he saw a shambling form emerging from the mist.

Darrell still shouted accusations and insults, his face puce with rage, but Drew blocked out the words, focusing instead on the malevolent movement behind his leader. Instinct told Drew to shout a warning, but something else, born of vengeful resentment, sealed his lips.

"Why are you smiling, boy?" Darrell asked.

Teeth sank into Darrell's shoulder. Screaming, he turned clumsily, shotgun falling to the ground. He threw an off-balanced punch into the thing's dead face, and the creeper stumbled backward.

Two more forms emerged from the gloom. One tore an arm, the other, crouching low, a leg.

Then there were more.

Darrell wailed as a throng of creepers, multiplying out of the fog, descended on his crumpling, viscera-coated form. His screams didn't last long.

When hungry maws found Drew, he was still smiling.

———

In the light of the moon, The Hunter sat in the tree-stand, gripping the handle of the tranquilizer gun—a weapon Mother had insisted he order, and now he knew why. Strapped across his back was his trusty deer rifle, just in case the tranquilizer darts didn't work on the flesh-eaters. He scanned the space around him for Mother's assurance the darts would work, but she was nowhere to be seen or heard; she hadn't been around ever since he'd changed. The fog was starting to abate, giving him greater visibility. Gazing toward the night sky, stars now faintly perceptible, he silently thanked his Maker.

He felt sad for what happened to Ginny and the kids, but *it*, what made him who he was now, couldn't have been avoided. The herd had to be culled; it was God's plan. And The Hunter was not one to question the will of The Lord. Still, he wished they'd been spared, to help him with his work.

In the distance, he heard voices—dead, hungry voices—and wet uneven footsteps. *Flesh-eaters.* Two forms appeared in the clearing below—one tall, a male, and the other short, a female. The male was leading, his female lagging behind a few paces. It was the female who was making most of the noise, her grunts and cries echoing through the woods like some kind of demonic mating call.

With the male's head in the crosshairs, The Hunter squeezed the trigger.

Hit, the flesh-eater ran in circles, his female chasing after him, wailing like a wounded cow. Soon, the large flesh-eater fell to the ground, moaning and trembling. The female shuffled to his side.

The Hunter was surprised by her display of devotion,

watching the scene with the rapt attention of a child at the circus. He reloaded the gun with a fresh dart and, lining the female's torn neck in the cross-hairs of the scope, fired.

Whiz, smack. The dart made contact. But she seemed oblivious to it. She continued to shake her trembling mate, howling. After a couple minutes she slumped across his still form.

He waited, just to be sure the flesh-eaters were out cold, and then tucked his tranquilizer gun into his shoulder holster and climbed down from his perch.

He trundled a wheelbarrow from behind the tree he'd been in and then snapped plastic gloves onto his hands. Loading the bodies, one on top of the other, he scanned the woods for movement. Satisfied he was safe, he gripped the implement's handles and began pushing.

The ground was wet, and getting them back to the house was hard work. But it wasn't far. And hard work wasn't a problem; after all, he *was* The Hunter.

––––––––––––

Geoff had only gone a few miles past the state line of Arkansas when he lost control of the SUV. Around a sharp bend, there was a loud pop, and the vehicle began to fight him. He steered into the skid, then, his tires gaining purchase, steered back. He slammed on the brakes and fell forward, hitting his head against the steering wheel.

A dull ache spread through his neck, his vision clouding. With a few deep breaths, he steeled himself against passing out. The indicator lights on his dashboard signaled a flat tire. He banged his clenched fists against the steering wheel. Then he reached deep for control. The situation wasn't hopeless; there had to be a solution. He wasn't going to give in like he'd done all his life. He was going to fight.

He pulled the SUV to the side of the road, metal screeching against wet pavement. He cut the ignition, grabbed his keys, and got out.

The night air smelled strangely clean as he walked to the back of his vehicle and opened the hatch. The gas containers had moved around but none of them had fallen. He tossed two empty containers aside and then heaved the remaining three out of the back, placing them on the ground. That's when he noticed the bumper was shattered in the middle and remembered the second gunshot from the redneck roadblock. He pulled open the door to the spare tire and almost broke down.

The spare had been punctured by the shot.

He put the gas containers back in place, grabbed his toolkit, and slammed the hatch shut. He pressed the lock button on his key chain, and the two beeps from the security mechanism made him feel foolish. *For fuck's sake, there are two broken windows.*

He took a deep breath and closed his eyes. "Please God," he said. "Watch over this gas while I'm away. Please...for Amanda. And please help me stay serene. I can't help her if I lose it. Amen." He wasn't a religious man, though he'd been raised Catholic. But now, prayer seemed apropos. What was the old aphorism? *There are no atheists in foxhole*s. He nodded. The expression certainly fit his situation.

Amanda's smiling face a beacon in his mind's eye, Geoff began walking southward, following the path of the road. He was in the sticks, but would come across a vehicle soon. He had to—it was his only hope.

His brother, Ray, had taught him how to hotwire a car when he'd been thirteen. Ray had been halfway through the second year of a four-year stretch in Leavenworth when The October Blast had hit. Geoff didn't like to think about that. He was sure Ray was dead, if he'd been lucky. But it didn't matter; Ray had been dead to him for years.

"Thanks, Ray," he muttered, looking up at the clear night sky. "You were a monster, but at least you taught me one useful skill." And then, despite the grim situation he was in, he laughed, remembering a brief but warm moment with Ray.

94

The night was unnaturally quiet. No birds. No bugs.
No—

The silence was broken by a nearby rustling. He froze,
his heart in his throat.

A deer galloped into the road and then stopped.

Geoff jerked back with a gasp, raising the toolkit as a
weapon.

Head tilted, the deer studied him, appearing not to be
intimidated. "The balance is shifting," the deer said.

Eyes wide, Geoff dropped the toolkit to the ground.

The deer's gaze shifted to the other side of the tree-
lined road. It stood impossibly still—not a blink, not a
tremor, not a breath—then sprang into the woods.

Geoff crouched low to the ground, fighting to regain
composure. *You're losing it. Man up!* He slowly stood.
Pushing the notion of a talking deer from his mind, he
started walking. The tremors in his extremities began to
calm as he concentrated on his purpose. Amanda. He had
to remain single-minded, he reminded himself. Fear, pain,
doubt—avoid them all, block them out. "Amanda," he
said, her name echoing through his mind like a mantra.

It wasn't long before he reached a crooked mailbox
labeled JENKINS. Next to the mailbox was a gravel
driveway that wound into the distance. Following the path
to the Jenkins' residence, his heart soared with hope. The

house drew nearer, dim light flickering through slats in the basement windows. Parked in front of the house was a rusted Ford F-150 that looked like it might have been red in better days. *As long as it runs, I'm golden.*

He crept to the truck and said a silent prayer it would be unlocked. He popped the door handle slowly and smiled. With a click and a rapid *ding-ding-ding*, the door came open. He jumped inside, slowly pulled the door shut, and slung his toolkit onto the passenger seat. He snatched a flat-head screwdriver and a hammer from the kit, stuck the head of the screwdriver into the ignition, and began to pound the screwdriver's handle with the hammer.

A shadow fell over him.

He glanced up, coming face-to-face with a bearded, wild-eyed man. Geoff reached for the door-lock but was too late.

The man jerked the door open. "What the fuck you doin', boy?" he shouted.

Geoff tried to explain, but before his mouth could form words, the butt of the bearded man's handgun came down on his head.

The world went dark.

———

Bathed in flickering candlelight, the dank cellar evoked the distant notion of ritual—religious or otherwise, memory eluded her. She gripped cold, rusty bars and, looking into the adjoining cage, waited for a sign of his affection for her. When alive, he had uttered her three favorite words as a matter of routine. But the power of speech now gone, for her and for him, she was left staring into his pallid eyes, the comfort of words an impossible dream.

Had there ever been sincerity in his eyes? She couldn't remember. She couldn't recall her name, her parents, or her job. Precious little survived The October Blast. But she knew she'd loved him, and that he'd been her reason for living. She still loved him, even though they were dead.

From upstairs came the clomping of footsteps and the squeal of something, or probably someone, being dragged across linoleum. She looked at the empty cage to her right and knew it would soon be occupied. Her captor—their captor—the man who called himself The Hunter, had undoubtedly trapped another of their kind in the woods.

Why didn't he kill them? Why did he prolong their suffering—her suffering? His plan, if he had one, was a mystery to her. But she knew he was insane and growing crazier with every passing minute.

The cellar door was flung open with a bang. "Goddamn this fucker's heavy," The Hunter moaned. Carrying a body over his shoulder, he gingerly descended the creaky stairs. His balance lost for a moment, his new prisoner's head thudded against the wooden railing of the—

She smelled blood immediately. Not the blood of her kind. *Living blood!* A deep guttural noise erupted from her throat and with it came hunger; not the type of hunger she'd known when alive—predacious compulsion, a product of her reanimated and unstable nervous system, not her gut or brain. Her reactions were involuntary, impossible to resist.

To her left, the man she loved rattled the bars of his cage violently. His maw of dirty jagged teeth and black gums, a passage for high-pitched shrieks, grew wide. His desire for flesh—his desire for anything not her—was a reminder of his cold indifference toward her affection. A wave of sorrow staggered her, made her forget for an instant her dark nature, her need to feed.

The Hunter didn't place the man in a cage. He laid him on a cot at the opposite end of the room and tied his hands and feet to the cot's rusty posts. Finished with the knots, he inspected his work. "What the hell were you doing on my property?" he shouted, shaking the breather by the shoulders.

The new prisoner moaned and fidgeted but didn't wake to respond.

A sneer on his face, The Hunter turned to face her.

"Hello, darlin'. Ain't you hungry?" His sneer became a wicked grin as he approached.

She averted his stare, looking down at the filthy floor of her cage. Something metallic clanked the bars above her head and when she looked up it was into the barrel of a pistol. She leaned forward, putting her forehead as close to the gun as she could.

The Hunter backed away, clearly afraid of being scratched or bitten. She pled with her eyes and tried to find her voice. But all that came from her mouth was a feral whine.

The Hunter cackled. Holding the gun up, he squeezed off a shot. The blast rang through the small space, dust fell from the ceiling, and smoke billowed from his gun. Ears ringing, senses frayed, she fell backward.

Her love hunched in the corner of his cage, the corner nearest hers. Reaching out, she stroked his thick, matted hair. She was glad for the contact, even though he didn't respond to her touch, only trembled as the painful echoes of gunfire rang through their heads.

"Gunshots are like tranquilizers to you freaks, ain't they?" The Hunter asked.

The breather on the cot muttered, "Amanda, I'm coming...spare," and began to move his arms and legs futilely against the restraints.

"But, damn, ain't no better way to wake the living."
The Hunter smiled. Holding the gun outward, he strode
toward his breathing captive. "What the hell were you
doing on my property?"

The breather coughed and then, a grimace of pain on
his face, shook his head weakly. "I-I had a blowout...about
a mile down the road...I was...I didn't know if anyone lived
here, but I saw a light on...I was...scared."

"And what in God's name are you doing out here in
the middle of nowhere anyway? You look like a fuckin' city
boy to me."

The breather nodded. "Omaha."

"Omaha? Shit boy, that's hundreds of miles away. And
where was you tryin' to get?"

"Memphis."

"Memphis! That's more'n a hundred miles from here.
What are you, boy...stupid? With all the shit going down,
you expect me to believe you headed into the hills of
Arkansas clear down from Nebraska? Did you think you
could just pull into a Phillips 66 and fill your damn tank?"

"I brought plenty of gas, and I'd...I'd be happy to share,
but I don't have a spare tire. I promised Amanda I'd go to
her...before the power cut out...before the...the lines all
went dead. I...gave my word. I love her."

Ears pricked by the man's statement of devotion, she

100

reached her arms through the bars of the cage. "Curregh aargh," she wailed, trying to say, "*Let him go.*"

The breather's head bolted up, his eyes locked with hers. "Christ, you have fucking zombies down here?" Now frantic, he struggled to break free from his restraints.

The Hunter laughed. "Settle down. You ain't got no room to judge, son. And don't call 'em zombies. Zombie means they don't know what they're doing. These fuckers are flesh-eaters."

"Okay. Flesh-eaters!"

"That's better, but it still don't explain why, with all these fuckin' flesh-eaters about, you risked your neck. You expect me to believe it's all for some floozy?"

"Don't call her that. I came because I made a promise, because—"

"I know, I know, 'cause you *love* her. Well I got news for you, numb-nuts, love died when the world died. Love died with my wife and children. Love died with The Blast, when the dead started shamblin' 'round, feedin' on the unlucky survivors. The New World Order has arrived, and The Hunter—that's me!—is gonna make the rules."

"We still...we still outnumber them."

"You think? Did you get that from CNN or the newspaper? Oh yeah, I was forgetting; ain't no more TV and ain't no more papers. If we outnumber the dead, then why the hell are they winning?"

"But why...why keep them down here? Why not kill them?"

"And what, set them free? That ain't justice. No, no...I make 'em suffer. I let 'em starve."

"In aid of what?"

"In aid of...Boy, you are stupid. Retribution for their sins, what else?"

The one she loved was again ravenous, rattling the bars of his cage. But she remained calm, gazing upon the lovesick breather with something akin to pity.

"You have no qualms with me," the prisoner said. "Let me go, so I can get to her."

The Hunter seemed to contemplate the request for a moment and then answered, "Nope."

A look of shock registered on the young man's face. "But...but why?"

"Keepin' you down here, a little out of reach, makes my guests...*hungry*, you know? And the hungrier I keep 'em, the more they suffer. Sorry, boy, that's just how the cookie crumbles. But don't worry, I ain't heartless. I'll feed ya, and I won't hurt ya too bad. Gotta draw blood every now and then, just to keep the scent alive, but—"

"You don't understand. She's lost touch with her family in Lincoln, she's worried—"

"No, *you* don't understand. I...don't...care."

The trapped breather wept, his body racked by spasms.

A tear fell from her eye, a warm rivulet sluicing and burning down her cold, dead cheek. Something bubbled deep inside her—a strange mixture of hunger, rage, and compassion. She closed her eyes, and a happy memory flooded back...

...California. The beach. Joe—she suddenly remembered his name—was behind her, holding her waist, both of them resting in the warm sand. Warmth. The world was still in color. The sun was setting, and a cool breeze blew in from the ocean.

"I love you," Joe said.

She turned her head and looked into his eyes.

It had been there before. Love. Maybe it had died with The Blast. But it had been there before! And if it was there before...

Eyes still closed, she lunged forward. The bars of the cage tore into her flesh, but she felt no pain. She reared back, eyes again open to her sepia-toned hell, and charged forward a second time. The bone in one arm snapped in half, and something else broke...something in the lock. She backed up and slammed against the door again.

The door flew open.

The Hunter drew his weapon clumsily and fired a shot. A red bloom appeared on her chest, and the bullet pounded painlessly into her ribcage. She staggered back from the impact, but soon, intent on her prey, she regained her footing, the shot reverberating painfully through her head. The Hunter's second shot missed her entirely. Her teeth sank into his arm, and his pistol clanked against the crumbling cellar floor.

She could hear the human prisoner scream and struggle against his bonds.

Her serrated teeth plunged into The Hunter's neck. His screams deteriorated to garbled, gargling cries, blood spewing from his mouth.

A sensation of warmth raced through her nervous system. Strength. Euphoria. Her bleak world was replenished with bright, pulsating colors. Chewing the flesh of The Hunter's warm, tender throat, she took satisfaction in watching the life ebb from his fearful eyes. She would finish him later, she thought. She still needed to deal with the breather on the cot.

"Please," he cried. "Please don't..."

She held up her hands, trying to convey benevolent intent. But the man's body continued to quake, his eyes alive with fear. Working slowly, she used her good hand to untie the restraints. It was not an easy task, but eventually he was free of his bonds. Despite his newfound range of motion, he remained frozen.

She backed away from the young man, giving him a wide berth and pointed to The Hunter's gun on the floor, emphasizing the action she wanted him to take—the action he needed to take—by jabbing a stiff finger forward repeatedly.

He finally looked where she pointed. Still trembling, he managed a nod. He gingerly got up from the cot and picked up the pistol.

Pointing up at the cellar door, she urged him to leave.

He looked confused. "Why...why are you letting me go?"

She put her hand on her chest and sighed. She could only imagine what that must have looked like through his eyes.

Behind her, Joe thrashed against the bars of his cage, trying to free himself as she had. Frustrated by his impatience, she shot him an angry glare. And with a defeated groan, he seemed to relent.

She motioned toward the stairs again, catching her reflection in a cracked mirror that hung next to a boarded window. Her decomposing lips were turned into a dreadful grimace of decaying gums and jagged teeth. Her neck was bloated and torn open.

Ashamed and horrified by her appearance, she looked away. No wonder the man was frightened. She was a monster.

When she turned her attention back to the breather, he was running, tripping up the stairs. Once he was gone from view, she listened to him fumble around on the main floor of the house—drawers and doors opening, the clanging of metal, and frantic footfalls. After a few moments, a door slammed, and then the loud roar of The Hunter's truck, peeling out as fast as the engine could go. Certain the breather was safely away, she fished a set of keys from The Hunter's pocket.

She freed Joe, and they dined.

———

Trees swayed and indistinct forms melted into one another. Geoff sensed zombie presence; he could hear and smell them. He studied the large run-down brick house with white columns, the place to which Amanda had fled.

Two forms shambled onto the porch of the house.

Amanda's rescue wasn't going to be easy. Nothing ever was. Thank God he'd stocked up at The Hunter's.

Geoff gripped the 9mm in his right hand and stepped out of the truck. He snatched the revolver from the dashboard and tucked it into his waistband. From the bed of the truck he grabbed an AA-12 assault shotgun, clipped on the 20-shell drum, and strapped the gun across his back. Turning to face the house, he saw the two zombies stepping off the porch, growling and grunting as they advanced. Geoff started walking. He leveled the 9mm, taking aim at one of them—a thin male in a V-neck sweater. A quick blast and recoil, and a dark bloom appeared on the thing's head. The second zombie—Hardy to the other's Laurel—covered his ears, one of them mangled and hanging by a thin thread of blackened flesh. Hardy shrieked as Geoff took aim. A squeeze of the trigger took the porcine zombie down.

Adrenaline pumping, Geoff tried the front door. It was locked. Scanning the mailboxes, he looked for Amanda's name. Found it. *Travis Stillwell & Amanda Herbert - Unit B, south side terrace.* "Travis," he muttered with contempt. Then, remembering Travis was dead, he smiled.

He jumped off the porch and then crept along the south wall of the house. In the distance, he saw a door with a large "B" stenciled on it; a few yards down from that was a carport with a VW Bug parked inside. Crouched by one of the Bug's wheels was a short, fat female with dreadlocked hair, half her face missing. One hand was splayed awkwardly against the car for balance.

She glanced in his direction and moaned.

He fired. The back window of the Bug shattered. She rose on stiff legs and began moving toward him. He took a step forward, steadied, and fired again.

Her head blew back and she crumpled to the ground like a rag doll.

But the moans of the dead didn't cease. From behind the carport *they* crawled and shambled. Geoff's eyes went wide, his pulse quickening. He took two steps back to give himself more room and surveyed the size of the enemy.

Half a dozen of them, moving with dead determination.

He dropped the 9mm to the ground and swung the shotgun off his back. Planting the butt of the gun on his shoulder, he took aim at the closest zombie—a man in a business suit, chattering his teeth as if demonstrating his new dentures. Geoff pulled the trigger, and the top half of Businessman's head exploded in a spray of gore.

Geoff was in awe; he'd never fired anything so powerful with such minimal recoil. Lord only knew what dark alley deal had landed the gun in The Hunter's arsenal, but—*Fuckin' A!*—he was glad of it.

The other five were going crazy, shrieking and wailing. They didn't seem to like the report from the AA-12. He opened fire on them, keeping the gun level with their heads as he mowed them down, guessing what they might have been—school teacher, bartender, drug dealer, truck driver, and cop. The last one was easy, he was in uniform.

His ears ringing from the multiple blasts, he lowered

the shotgun.

Suddenly, he was pushed from behind.

He fell to the muddy earth, dropping the AA-12. Instinctively, he rolled onto his back just in time to see a tall female zombie in a sequined club-dress lunging at him.

He moved out of the way as she splashed face-first into the mucky earth. Getting back on his feet, he pulled the revolver from his belt and took aim at Party-girl's head. A quick bang and she, too, was gone.

He rearmed himself with the shotgun, made a three hundred sixty degree inspection of his surroundings, and then, strapping the AA-12 around his back, rushed to Amanda's door and knocked.

No answer. Thinking of her, against his better judgment, he aimed the revolver at the deadbolt. "Stand back, Amanda!"

A quick blast splintered the door open.

Hearing a sucking noise behind him, he spun around. Three more zombies were advancing. He dispatched the first two quickly—a skinny teen with a missing arm and a burly oaf with a missing jaw. But the third squeeze of the trigger only produced a dry, hollow click.

He ducked into the apartment. "Amanda," he shouted. "We have company. Wake up."

He turned to face the zombie in the doorway—a short

teenage boy wearing a T-shirt emblazoned with the slogan *FIVE DOLLAR FOOTLONG* and an arrow pointing to his crotch. Geoff brought the shotgun around and fired.

Footlong's head splattered across the door, and his body toppled into the apartment.

He assumed that the other dead guy in the living room, the one with the iron rod sticking out of his skull, was Travis.

The first light of dawn bled through the open doorway. The temperature gauge by the front window read 105 degrees.

Why didn't the zombies break through the window?

The question terrified him.

Part of a televised interview with a doctor from the CDC came back to him with an answer: "*From what we have observed, the reanimated corpse is only attracted to living blood and tissue.*"

Racing for the hallway, he began to cry. The first room was small—desk, computer, a couple stacks of books. The next room—king mattress, a framed *Led Zeppelin* poster, a bookshelf with a bong on top of it.

His body drenched in sweat, he held his breath. He made the sign of the cross: forehead, chest, left shoulder, right shoulder.

And then, slowly, he opened the bathroom door...

When Joe fled into the woods, she didn't go after him. It was clear the spark that had caused him to love her once had been frozen to oblivion in The Blast. Wanting her pain to be at an end, she took to the road, exposing herself to would-be hunters.

The sun was coming up when she heard a vehicle approach from the south. She turned and saw The Hunter's truck speeding around a corner. It slowed as it passed, and then pulled over a few yards in front of her.

Visibly distraught, the breather stepped out. He made his way to the back of the truck and lowered the tailgate, revealing two large gas containers and the corpse of a girl, not yet reanimated.

She wasn't sure what to do. Her instincts screamed for her to feed, a trace of fear asked her to flee, but her heart, or whatever it was that she was clinging to, told her to wait.

The breather kissed the dead girl's lips and muttered words she couldn't make out above the hot November wind. Tears in his eyes, he turned and approached.

"I was too late," he muttered. He held up The Hunter's gun and studied it, a deepening expression of grief in his sleepless eyes. "I know I should shoot her in the head...keep her from...from becoming like you, but I..." He tossed the gun into the nearby field and then crouched low, holding his head in his hands. "I can't do it," he screamed. "I won't do it!"

She stood motionless as he broke down at her feet.

"I always thought I tried too hard. But now I know that was a lie. I let the world happen to me. I never tried at all, not until now. Not until Amanda needed me." Finally, he looked up. "You let me go, so something...something human must still live inside you."

She shook her head.

"Don't deny it," he pleaded. "I know it's there."

Perhaps some vestige of humanity still lived in her at that point; she didn't know. But she didn't want the breather clinging to false hopes. She wanted him to flee, to leave her to others of his kind, to the hunters. To her end.

She shrieked sadly, waving her good hand, trying to get him to leave.

"Does love have to die?" he asked. "If it's strong enough, does it have to die when...when we die?"

She turned away from him, and a tear, the second she'd cried since her death, streamed down her cheek.

"It doesn't have to die, does it?"

Again, she shook her head. Maybe she was wrong to do it, but false hope, she decided, was better than no hope at all. She and Joe had died in The Blast. This young man and the girl he loved had survived, reaching out to each other across a long divide of terror. He had suffered, hadn't he? He had taken a risk that others would have considered reckless, even deplorable. Perhaps their love was strong, a thing that would endure, even in death.

The breather took her hand.

The urge to bite him was overwhelming, but she resisted it, her jaw clenched in defiance, her eyes shut against his presence.

He pulled one of her fingers to his face and, with a tightening grip, dug her nail into his cheek. Blood—hot, sticky, alive!—welled around her finger. She jerked away from him, sharp pains stabbing within, screaming at her to lunge, to tear, to rip, to rend, to—she folded her arms tightly and dropped to the gravel shoulder of the road, shaking violently, digging her bloody finger into the ground, attempting to deaden the intoxicating scent.

He must have sensed the urgency of her inner conflict because when she looked up the truck was racing toward the state line of Missouri.

By the side of the road, she waited.

Morning turned to day, day to night. But no cars came.

The next day, she joined the hordes in the woods.

She ran with others of her ilk; they hunted and fed on animals. But the animals were growing smarter, craftier every day, the Balance of Nature shifting. Many nights she went hungry, her corpse racked with want. She knew her kind didn't have long; it was clear the planet had plans for the future that didn't involve her. And as time passed—her flesh blackening, falling from her bones—she grew colder and colder inside as the world grew warmer. She even forgot about Joe. If she met him in the woods they would probably hunt in tandem, maybe even camp together for a while. But her feelings for him had gone as dead as her species.

Would her love have died had it been requited? Sometimes she thought not, other times she was not so sure; but mostly she didn't think about him at all. And yet, despite everything that she—that everyone—had lost, she never forgot the two breathers she'd tried to help.

Did their love survive?

She didn't know.

She knew the man had tried. They tried. And in the end, if there was anything she remembered about what she once was, if there was anything she clung to in the shining madness of the new world order, it was one simple truth.

We tried.

THE END

Finding Balance
—An Afterword—

After selling my first story—a tricky little number titled "The Better Half: A Love Story" that I wrote with Scott Bradley—to a professional anthology, edited by John Skipp, I said to myself, "Man, this being-a-writer thing isn't so tough!"

I was wrong. Oh, how I was wrong!

Not only did I have a hard time finding inspiration in the ensuing months, I found it even harder to sell the few stories I did write. I was frustrated! Having learned a few things about the biz now, I see what a baby I was being. But in that moment, I was sure my first fiction sale had been a fluke and that I would never publish another word.

During this time, I wrote a short story that I liked—that I still like—about a strange creature who encounters a young girl held captive in a cellar. It was called "Reaching for the Light." And the title expressed exactly how I felt.

It didn't sell.

But, for some reason, I couldn't shake the image of the girl in the cellar. I wanted to do something different with this cliché and thought there was a deeper story to be told than the ones I'd read or seen in movies.

Sometime later, I started writing a story aimed at Robert Essig's *Through the Eyes of the Undead II*. And I did something that I was pretty sure hadn't been done before, I made the girl in the cellar a zombie.

The story was called "Half Life" originally, and, for the most part, it is the finale of the novella you're holding in your hands.

And, damn, I was proud of that story!

In fact, I loved it!

So I sent it off to every friend I could think of who might want to read it. And many of them did.

It got a flurry of great responses, but with one consistent bit of criticism.

It needed to be longer. Everyone wanted to know what The Blast was. And everyone wanted to know more about the human relationships in the tale.

I was just glad they liked the story, so I sent it off to Robert. And he liked it, too! It looked like my short story was going to be accepted, and my dry spell would come to an end!

But in the weeks that followed, the feedback I had received from trusted friends rang through my head.

So I pulled up the story. Reread it a dozen times.

And damn it!

They'd all been right.

So I expanded "Half Life" into a novella called *The Blast*, pulled my story from Robert's wonderful antho, worried I'd lost my mind, and sent the new draft to Eric Shapiro, the most trusted of my readers and the person who'd given "Half Life" the biggest thumbs up! Surely, Eric was going to love this new, expanded version of a story he'd praised. I was on my way to becoming the master of the macabre! Delusions bloomed eternal on that day, my friends. They'll never die!

A few days later, I opened an email from Eric. I was excited and couldn't wait to hear how great I was.

I read his email and my jaw dropped.

He didn't think *The Blast* was so hot. He didn't hate it. But he didn't think it would resonate with readers or, for that matter, be published at all.

Though surprised, I made one of the best moves of my life. And writers, whether you're just starting out or have been doing this for decades, this is what we all need to do in these situations. Every time!

I asked him what was wrong with it. I asked him for details. I asked for help!

And he gave me what I asked for. And then his wonderful wife, Rhoda, read an improved version of the story and she gave me some more feedback.

So I fixed the story. And then I fixed it some more. Then…Well, you get the idea. I just kept fixing it until everyone—and by everyone, I mean Eric and Rhoda, who are two of the most wonderful people on the planet—loved it!

Then Eric gave me one last piece of advice. He told me *The Blast* sucked as a title. I asked him how bad it sucked, and he told me it sucked big. Really big!

I love my honest friends. If you're one of those friends who tells me what I want to hear then stop now! Unless I look really needy at the moment, if you want me to love you more, tell me what you really think.

I came up with *Balance*. And the moment that title entered my mind, I knew I had it. Why hadn't I thought of it sooner? I now can't imagine this story ever being called anything else, but when you're really close to something, it's easy to be blind.

Eric and Rhoda agreed with the title.

And so *Balance* was born.

Special thanks go to Eric Shapiro and Rhoda Jordan. They're busy people—making movies, writing books, building a family—and they certainly didn't have to take time out to help me. But they did. And I'm forever in their debt.

I learned a lot working with them. I learned to give a little more.

So in the spirit of giving a little more, I thought it would be fun to give you, dear reader, the original short story "Reaching for the Light," never before published, in this EJP edition of *Balance*.

I hope you enjoy it.

—Peter Giglio / Lincoln, Nebraska / 12 -26 - 2011

REACHING FOR THE LIGHT

The code of his kind was simple—stay away from humans and things of their making and hunt at night. The latter he was fine with, but Glom's curiosity, a peculiarity which earned him many harsh words from elder dwellers, made the first rule in the code hard to obey. Despite rebukes, he felt no shame for his rebellion; rather, he was ashamed of his breed—easily scared, overly suspicious, and perpetually closed-minded.

At an age between education and family, free to hunt in the woods to his stomach's content, he was in his prime. "The years of building strength," elders called it.

Nonsense, he thought, *my culture is as nourishing as the muck in which we dwell.*

He needed more—adventure, romance, mystery—things he'd discovered in books written by humans; sweeping, lyrical tales discarded to his delight in large green bins behind ominous, gray buildings. He savored every word, even though much of what he read was dense and hard to understand. And his obsession was risky. If discovered with the prose of light-walkers, the penalty would be unspeakable. Which was why, he assumed, it went unspoken.

Peering around a tree, he watched the tall, gray-haired

man speed away in a shiny, black box.

This man's house, nestled in a clearing, often fed Glom's voyeuristic appetite, and he knew the dark man as the sole occupant. The home—a sharp, castle-like monstrosity—possessed the spoils of Glom's desire, basking in dim, yellow light behind ornately latticed windows—shelves and shelves of precious books, begging discovery within each page.

Glom scuttled through snow, struggled up slick, wooden stairs, and then waddled to a tall, transparent door. He touched the door and knew it was secured—the locking mechanism clear in his mind's eye, lending credence to myth.

According to legend, his people defeated locks with the power of thought. His kind didn't employ locks in their holes, so he'd never had the chance to test the myth, but now, with the lock so clear in his brain, the tales were starting to ring true.

Often speaking of his breed's nature, his father warned, "Greed led to our discovery. Man called us 'Ghoul' and hunted us down with merciless brutality. To survive, we forsook our gift and trade. In their eyes, we were evil incarnate. As we deepened our homes, hunting only in the small hours of darkness, many generations of man thought us extinct. Now, they've forgotten us completely."

Glom concentrated on the bolt, further testing the elders' fables. When a dull click sounded, he gasped in ecstasy. Sliding the door open as he'd seen the dark man do several times before, he smiled. Generations bridged, he felt close to his ancestors, in touch with his roots. Though giddy beyond words, he forced his legs to remain still, though the urge to dance was strong. Celebration could wait, he told himself, and embarking upon alien terrain called for prudence. He would need to resist greed, too. He'd only take one book.

Maybe two.

And, though thievery burned in his veins, he would return what he took before *borrowing* more.

As he snatched a heavy tome from a low shelf, a high-pitched cry pricked his ears.

He jerked away from the wall of riches and scanned his moonlit environs for animals. Though he'd never spied pets through the windows, he yanked the crossbow from his back and sprang into a defensive crouch. Better safe than sorry.

The second time he heard the cry, he recognized it as human.

Reverently, he slid the book back in place.

Walking down a spiral staircase, terror enveloped him. Part of his will, bent on self preservation, screamed *Leave!*

But, distinguishing himself from other dwellers—other "Ghouls"—he fought the temptation to flee. With each step he took, frightening sounds grew louder.

Chains rattled. Nails clawed.

And an unpleasant odor intensified.

Fear, sweat, blood, and sex.

When he reached the base of the staircase he was surprised to find the sounds and scents still further below him.

The house had another level.

A secret level?

Soon, he found a secured passageway and unlocked it with his mind. He swung the door open, and the acrid stench intensified, making his eyes water. Urgent warnings sounded in the reptilian depths of his brain, but mystery drew him down.

One to admire stories of bravery and people in distress, he recognized his situation. An act of heroism might—*would*—elevate the status of his sorry lot, he thought. Not that they held any standing to speak of in the world of human affairs.

"I'll be able to walk in the light," he whispered. "We all will."

"Who's there?" someone shouted.

The voice belonged to a girl, and he could tell she'd

been weeping.

He tried to speak, but words choked in his throat.

Plodding down the stairs, he reached up to the metal railing for support. He was on the verge of breaking the most sacred rule of his people. Power stirred inside him.

I'm doing the right thing, he told himself.

The calloused pads of his feet met cold concrete. He took a deep breath and found his voice. "I'm…here to… help."

"Thank God," the girl said with a glint of happiness in her otherwise sad tone. "Are you a cop?"

Glom stepped into a slash of moonlight that bled through a thin rectangular window. He didn't know what a cop was, but he was pretty sure he wasn't one. He shook his head and turned to face the girl.

She screamed.

He jerked back and took a closer look at her.

She was beautiful—long orange hair, alabaster skin, full lips.

And she was hurt—a deep cut across her cheek, body heavily bruised, bloody gashes on her legs. Around each ankle, thick metal bands dug into her flesh.

Her screams subsiding, fear still danced in her emerald eyes.

"What…what the hell…are you?"

He tilted his head and smiled, trying to look valiant. "A friend," he proclaimed proudly.

"I've gone mad. Christ, I'm fucking seeing things."

Unsure what to make of her response, he gently touched her shoulder.

She screamed again.

"Calm yourself," he said in a thin voice. His rough hand trailed down her smooth arm. "I'm here to help you."

"How can you help me? You're fucking two feet tall. And there's no way you're real."

He stood as straight as possible, fighting the natural curvature of his back. "I'll have you know that I stand nearly three feet high, one of the tallest of my clan." He tried to sound proud but knew himself a failure.

She cackled wildly. "So what's your goddamn name?"

"I am Glom. And what do they call you?"

"My parents named me Rita. But most know me as Angel—that's my stage name."

"Are you an actress?" His eyes widened in awe.

She smiled crookedly, revealing a missing front tooth. "Somethin' like that."

A wave of exhilaration embraced him.

This girl, someone special, would tell the world of his nobility, and people would listen. They'd have to listen to someone special.

Unable to curb his delight, he broke into a jig and thought, *what a glorious way to make our way back into the light.* All the others would have him to thank. He'd be a hero for sure!

"For fuck's sake," Angel moaned.

Suddenly self-conscious, Glom stopped dancing and was troubled by a flurry of thoughts.

Why is she down here? Did she do something to warrant punishment? Something…wrong?

He'd heard humans were cruel and read several stories in which they actually killed their own. But he'd never completely believed the stories. They were just so…so unbelievable. Now he started to believe.

"Have you committed a crime, Angel?"

She shook her head. "Not exactly."

"Then why are you chained to the wall?"

"You must be kidding me. The man who keeps me down here is crazy."

"Crazy?"

"Insane. Not right in the head. He gets off by torturing girls. He drugged me then brought me down here. Do I need to draw you a fuckin' map?"

Depravity too deep to grasp, confusion swept Glom's face.

"There must be others like you," she said.

He nodded.

"Well, aren't some of them crazy?"

"No. I don't…think so…" His mind drifted…

Flickering candlelight, mother warming herself by the clay oven. He, only a youngling, stared up with wide hopeful eyes and asked, "Why do we hate the light-walkers?"

She turned and sneered. "They hunted our kind for generations. And now they defile our mother, filling the air with toxins and poisoning the streams. We are weak because of them. Were we stronger, we'd rise up and destroy them. But we know it's not necessary. They're killing themselves, and in time we will once again walk in the light."

"Father showed me what they look like the other night."

"Oh?"

"We watched from the edge of the woods. I think they look nice."

"You're crazy to say that, and far too young to be at the edge of the woods." She stomped her feet in anger.

"So, you gonna help me or stare at me all day?" Angel asked.

Crazy…

"I'm sorry…I…"

Crazy…

"I'm here to…help."

Crazy!

A loud mechanized clanking followed by a feral roar came from above.

"Jesus, he's back," Angel cried.

Glom concentrated on the locks of Angel's shackles, unable to visualize their inner-workings. He knelt low, held her ankles in his hands, and caressing the cold metal bands.

"What the fuck are you doing?" she shouted, kicking her legs and slapping him with her hands.

"Be still," he said. "I'm trying to defeat the locks."

"How?"

"With my mind."

"You're crazy."

He stood, tears trailing down his green face. "I am not."

A door slammed shut, and then heavy footsteps thumped above.

Glom's heart raced.

Crazy…

He'd soon be discovered.

Crazy…

His people would once more be hunted. And it was his fault.

"Are you gonna get me out of here or what?"

The cellar door creaked opened.

"Angel," the dark man boomed. "*Darling*, what seems to be the matter?"

A light came on as Glom scurried beneath a table.

"Let me go," Angel cried.

The man laughed, clomping down the stairs.

Glom aimed the crossbow forward, nodding in Angel's direction. Bathed in the unnatural light, her wounds looked gruesome. Sitting in a pool of blood, she continued to kick, muscle and nerve exposed where the restraints had torn into her flesh.

Again, Glom focused on her bonds.

One of her legs kicked free, an open shackle clanking against the floor.

The man stepped in front of her. "What the—"

Glom sprang forward, aimed upward, and released the arrow from the bow as the man turned.

Thwap!

The arrow sank into the soft human neck.

With a sudden jerk, the man screamed then kicked Glom.

Glom's world spun.

He hit the floor hard, nasty pinpricks radiating through his forearms and short, wide legs. He shook his head rapidly, trying to summon his wits. His sight was fuzzy, telescoping in and out wildly. But then a loud blast cleared his head for him.

He dashed aimlessly in serpentine patterns, objects exploding around him.

Suddenly, something smashed his leg with the force of a thousand raging dwellers in heat, pulling the floor from under Glom. Headfirst, he collapsed, flares of white hot pain spiking through his entire body.

Squinting from agony, he could see the upside-down man looming above him.

A river of blood ran down the man's neck, and it looked like he, too, was fighting to keep his eyes open.

"What the...what the fuck are you?" the man asked. Lips quivering, he sneered then, before Glom could respond, crumpled to the floor.

"Bring me his gun!" Angel shouted.

Pain intensified as Glom pried the metal object from the human's hand; his eyes burned from the acrid smoke billowing from the object's muzzle. "This?" he muttered, holding the cold, hard thing up.

"Yeah, bring it to me. Now!"

Weak, he crawled toward her, blood gushing from his shattered leg. He handed her the fearsome implement then watched her aim it at the remaining chain. After two earsplitting bangs, she was free.

Glom reached out to her as she limped toward the

stairs. "Please...I need a healer."

She turned. "You and me both, buddy."

"I don't live far from here. Carry me into the woods. The healer will fix us both...I promise...not far...I can't make it by myself."

"Sorry, you're on your own now."

"Please...I saved you...I—"

"I don't even know what you are, what diseases you carry, and you expect me to pick you up?"

"My kind lives underground. We fear humans...but mean you no harm."

She laughed. "You should have stayed underground. Look at you—you're hideous. Lord only knows what they'll make of you when they find you here."

"So you'll be sending someone?"

"Hell no. I know where the fucker keeps his money, and once I've taken what's rightfully mine, I'll never breathe a word about what happened here."

Tears ran down Glom's cheeks. Angel ran up the stairs.

He held onto consciousness for as long as he could and thought about the code.

Stay away from humans.

Now he knew why. Just as Mother had warned, they were crazy.

Just like him.

Life ebbing, he closed his eyes. He imagined himself walking in the light.

And then he was.

————

It was the smell of home—dank earth, unwashed kinsmen fresh from the hunt, roasting deer meat—that told him he was alive. He slowly opened his eyes to find Cleng, the senior elder, looking down with surprisingly benevolent eyes.

"I'm glad to see you awake," Cleng said.

"How did I—"

"Your mother's been tracking your scent through the woods at night. It seems she's been worried about you. You were delivered to the healers just in time."

Glom sat up and began to rub his sore leg. "What you must think of me—saved by my mother like a helpless cub."

"She tells me you've been reading human words."

Glom's blood ran cold. Trembling, he turned to face the elder. "How does she know?"

"It is not my place to question the intuition of a mother. I take it her words are true?"

Glom nodded. "And the punishment?"

Cleng laughed. "It's more common a crime than you think. When I was your age, I had a fascination with Greek mythology. I was particularly fond of a story about a fellow named Icarus. His father, a skilled craftsman, built wings made of feathers and wax. He warned his son not to fly too close to the sun. But Icarus didn't heed his father's words. The heat from the sun melted the wings, and Icarus fell to his death. It's okay to be curious, Glom. But it's never okay to fly too close to the sun. For now, we're just glad to have you back."

Glom considered the story for a moment.

"Do you understand?" Cleng asked.

"Yes," Glom muttered. But he knew his interpretation was different than the elder's. After all, he was crazy. Not crazy like the tall, gray-haired man, but crazy nonetheless. The type of crazy he could be proud of.

Smiling, Glom thought: *I need better wings next time!*

For the first time in more than 20 years…

New York Times Bestselling novelist Rick Hautala's first novel is
back in print! Featuring stunning cover art from the legendary
Glenn Chadbourne, and an all new introduction from
Christopher Golden, *Moondeath* is a must-have for any horror
fan!

"One of the best horror novels I've read in the last two years!"
– Stephen King (1980)

ISBN 13: 978-0615581026
ISBN 10: 0615581021
314 pages
Trade Paperback—$17.95
eBook—$3.99

AVAILABLE NOW FROM

HELP! WANTED
Tales of On-the-Job Terror

Available Now from Evil Jester Press!

Featuring stories by Stephen Volk, David Dunwoody, Lisa Morton, Gregory L.
Norris, Zak Jarvis, Adrian Chamberlin, Ellen Herbert, Patrick Flanagan, Gary
Brandner, David C. Hayes, Jeff Strand, Vince A. Liaguno, David Greske, Amy
Wallace, Vic Kerry, Henry Snider, Craig Saunders, Mark Allan Gunnells,
Marianne Halbert, Will Huston, Trevor Denyer, Matt Kurtz, Joe McKinney, Eric
Shapiro, and Scott Bradley.

Edited by Peter Giglio

Available from all major online retailers
Trade Paperback: $14.95
eBook: $4.99

ISBN 10: 0615536352
ISBN 13: 978-0615536354

Join the

 Evil Jester Press

F O R U M

Interact with authors and readers!
Stay informed about upcoming projects!
Tell us what you'd like to see from EJP!

It's Fun!

It's Free!

And The Jester's waiting for *you*!

Join the forum at:
www.eviljesterpress.lefora.com
And visit us at:
www.eviljesterpress.com